WANDERING MAN

A Novel of the McCabes

Brad Dennison

Author of
THE LONG TRAIL and *McCABE COUNY*

Published by Pine Bookshelf
Buford, Georgia

THE McCABES

The Long Trail
One Man's Shadow
Return of the Gunhawk
Boom Town
Trail Drive
Johnny McCabe
Shoshone Valley
Thunder
Wandering Man

JUBILEE

Preacher With A Gun
Gunhawk Blood (Coming Soon)

THE TEXAS RANGER

Tremain
Wardtown
Jericho (Coming Soon)

Cover Design: Donna Dennison

Editor: Martha Gulick

Copy Editor: Loretta Yike

PART ONE

The Mountains

1
June, 1883

Johnny stood in front of the cabin he shared with Jessica and the children. He had a tin cup of coffee in one hand, and he was watching Joe tie his soogan to the back of a horse. An axe was strapped across the top of his soogan, and a Winchester was in the saddle boot.

Years ago, when Johnny McCabe had been returning to Pennsylvania from Texas, he had found his brother Joe on the trail. Johnny hadn't seen him in more than two years.

Joe had always been the strongest of the four brothers, but Johnny found Joe was packed with even more muscle than ever. And his hair was long, touching his shoulders, and his face was covered with a thick, brown beard.

Now, more than twenty-five years later, Joe's hair was showing strands of gray, and his whiskers had a streak of white that touched his mustache and ran down the entire length of his jaw. Almost like someone had taken a brush with white paint, touched it to his upper lip and dragged it down the length of his beard.

His buckskin shirt wasn't the same one he had worn

back then. You can get only so many years out of one. But it didn't look much different. And he wore a floppy hat-again, not the same one from years ago, but like the original, the hat was a desert neutral color. He wore canvas pants that were tucked into black riding boots.

In the 1850s, Joe had worn a belt with a cap and ball Colt tucked into the front. Now he had a Peacemaker tucked into his belt. At his left side was a knife that was so long it looked like a short sword. The same knife he had always carried.

And he was still packed with solid muscle. The years hadn't taken that from him.

The sun hadn't yet showed itself, but the eastern sky was a steel gray. Johnny figured Joe would have a mile or two behind him before sunrise.

Morning birds were swooping about and filling the air with chatter and song.

Johnny said, "I hate to see you go. For years we didn't know where you were, or if you were even alive. But now I've gotten used to having you around."

"I'll be back. I just got the urge to roam. You know how it is."

Johnny nodded. "All too well."

The door opened as Johnny was speaking, and he looked over his shoulder to see Jessica. A robe was wrapped around her nightgown, and her hair was tied in a braid that fell down her back.

She said, "Joe. I hope you weren't just going to ride

off without giving us a chance to say goodbye."

He shrugged. "Ain't very good at goodbyes."

"Do you think you might go back to Texas?" Johnny said. "Work with Marshal Tremain again?"

"You never know. I just might. But he has Jericho Long working with him, and Doc Benson."

"The town doctor?"

"He's a doctor, but there's a lot more to him than that. He moves like a gunfighter and has the gunfighter look in his eye. He and Jericho are both men to ride the river with. With them at his side, Tremain will be all right."

Joe began tightening the cinch of his saddle. "So maybe I'll just roam the mountains for a while. Ride till I get the urge to roam out of my system."

Johnny held out his hand and Joe took it.

Johnny said, "Wherever you go, ride safe."

"I will. And you take care of this woman and them young'uns."

Joe pulled Johnny in for a back-slapping hug, and then Jessica stepped down from the porch and held her arms out. Joe gave her a hug.

He said, "You tell Eli that his Uncle Joe says he's turnin' into a good man. And Em is a good young lady, and Cora is turnin' into one, too."

Em was Joe's name for Melissa Jean. She was called M.J. by most everyone, and Joe had shortened it to Em. There were people in town calling her Emma, believing it to be her actual first name.

Joe turned away and grabbed a scattergun that had been leaning against the cabin wall. Though Joe kept a revolver tucked into his belt, the scattergun was his weapon of choice. He had taken a bullet through his right hand in Texas eight or nine years ago and he no longer had the strength in that hand to use a pistol.

He swung into the saddle. Two canteens were hanging from the saddle horn, and his soogan and saddlebags were in place. He traveled with only what he could carry on his horse. The way he had traveled when he first came back into Johnny's life.

Johnny and Jessica stood by a fence at the edge of the small shelf where the cabin stood, and from which they had a view of the canyon below. They watched as Joe rode toward the small rocky entrance to the canyon.

Thunder was at the canyon floor, grazing. He lifted his head and watched as Joe rode by.

Joe turned his horse through the small canyon entrance, and was gone.

Jessica said, "You said you knew what he meant about the urge to roam."

Johnny nodded his head. "If I had never had a family, I think I might have turned out very much like Joe. But I was blessed with the love of a good woman when I was younger, and now with another good woman."

"But Joe has never been so blessed."

Johnny shook his head. "There was a woman, a long

time ago. A Cheyenne girl he almost married. And there was that English woman he knew for only a few days, but the love between them was so strong you could almost feel it in the air."

Jessica nodded. "You told me about her. The one captured by Indians."

"Kate Waddell. In the course of only two days, she and Joe stole each other's heart. But she was promised to another man, and she was a woman of honor."

"That's so sad."

Johnny gave a slow nod of his head, his eyes on the canyon entrance that was now empty.

He said, "I forget the name of the man she was engaged to."

"I'll bet Joe remembers."

"I have no doubt. I remember his first name. Elias. He was from England, just like she was. But I forget his last name."

Johnny took Jessica's hand, and they stood in silence. He looked down at the canyon floor and then off at the mountains beyond, as the steel gray of the eastern sky transformed to summertime blue, and morning came to life.

2

Joe rode with no particular destination in mind. He let his horse have his head, and the horse wandered, drifting west and then south.

The horse was mountain-bred, which was what Joe wanted in a horse. This one was a buckskin, a little taller than the Indian pony he had been riding years ago, when he had been returning to Pennsylvania and found Johnny on the trail.

Johnny'd had more than his share of hardships over the years, Joe thought. But now he had Jessica, a good woman. While Johnny understood Joe's wanderlust, Joe figured Jessica never would. But she would try. That was something Joe respected.

That night, Joe made a campfire by a line of pines that overlooked a gully. A stream ran through the gully, because of winter runoff, but Joe figured in another month the stream would be mostly dry.

Joe knew this little area. He had camped here a couple of years before, when he took a weekend in the mountains for hunting.

He sat by the fire, thinking how good it was to be in the mountains again, just wandering. He had shot his supper, a rabbit that was roasting on a wooden spit he had cut with his knife.

He had only the supplies in his saddlebags and what

he could roll in his soogan. He had his rifle, his pistol and his long knife, and a smaller fold-up knife in a pocket of his buckskin shirt. Somehow, he felt at peace when he lived like this.

Johnny understood. Joe knew Matt did, too, even though Matt had never quite become a man of the wilderness like Joe and Johnny had.

Joe had supper a few nights earlier with Matt and Peddie, and he told them of his plans to depart. He got about the same reaction from them that he had from Johnny and Jessica.

Johnny had found love, first with Lura and then Jessica. He had a passel of children who ranged from Josh and Dusty, who were somewhere in their late twenties— Joe lost track of the years too easily and wasn't sure of their exact age—to the twins who were only two.

Eli was a good boy, who had passed fourteen a couple of months ago. He was a color that society would never accept, but he was a McCabe in every way that mattered.

Matt hadn't been as blessed as Johnny, getting himself snared by Verna McCarty years ago, but now he had the love of Peddie. She was almost young enough to be his daughter, but Joe figured that didn't matter none. What mattered was love.

Joe had found none of this for himself. He had come close a couple of times, but that was all he could claim. Not that he didn't think about that little Cheyenne gal once in a while. Or Kate Waddell.

The man Kate had married was from England, and though Joe would have liked to be in his place, Joe wished him no ill will.

The man's name was Elias Compton. Joe had heard the name once or twice over the years. A farmer out of Oregon who had done well. Gone into shipping and then various businesses. But Joe had never asked questions. He really didn't want to know. The less he knew about Kate's life with the Compton feller, the easier it would be for him to keep his thoughts away from her.

It worked most of the time, but not tonight. Not as he sat by the fire.

The rabbit was ready so he pulled it from the spit, and with a chunk of rabbit meat on his knife, he ate his supper.

As he was finishing off the rabbit, he heard the crack of a stick from somewhere off in the darkness. His horse was looking off in that direction, not really nervous but not too sure, either.

Joe grabbed his scattergun, with his left hand on the trigger. He wasn't a world-class shot using a gun with his left hand, but with a scattergun you didn't need to be. He stepped away from the fire, ready to shoot if he needed to.

He heard the patter of feet on dried leaves. Off behind the line of pines was a small grove of birch, and the sound was from that direction.

A critter, he figured. Maybe a wolf that had gotten

curious and was checking out the camp. Joe set his gun back on the ground, but kept it within reach.

He put a coffee kettle near the flames and waited for it to boil. He enjoyed the smell of campfire smoke, and of the coffee coming to life in the kettle. He loved the clean, mountain air and the sounds of the night. The crickets. The wind in the tree branches. Way off in the distance, almost too far away to hear, a wolf howled.

When the coffee was ready he filled a tin cup, and he sat and looked off into the night. He took a sip of the coffee, and he thought of Kate.

3

A week passed, and then another. Joe wandered out of the
Crazy Mountains and made his way south. He thought of
stopping in Bozeman, but decided against it.

He remembered before Bozeman was built, and
other towns like Helena, Billings and Bannack, and most
recently, Jubilee. Back when the Indians roamed the land,
living like they had for countless generations, and herds of
buffalo shook the Earth when they moved. Now the
Indians who hadn't been killed in wars against the Army
were confined to reservations, and the buffalo were gone.
All that was left from a time gone by was Joe.

White man towns and railroads were like a slap in
the face to Joe. A reminder that the world he had known
existed no longer. And so he passed by Bozeman.

He rode south for a while, sometimes through open
areas of grass and sage between mountain ridges, and other
times along ridge tops.

He turned east after a time, for no reason in
particular. After a couple of days, he turned south again.

The land opened up around him, stretching to the
horizon. Low, rolling hills, covered with green grass that
rippled in the wind. To the south and west, were ridges that
looked dark green and hazy in the distance. The
Absarokas.

He filled his canteen in the river known as the

Yellowstone. It was running fast with spring runoff.

It felt good to be out here again, he thought, as he rode along. The wind was strong and would sometimes shake the brim of his hat. Out here, the loneliness he lived with would seem to fall away.

And yet, there was a feeling of emptiness that had never been there before. This land was remote, but it had never before struck him as empty.

Then he realized what it was. There were no longer any war parties to watch out for. As a Cheyenne, or the closest a white man could come to being one, Joe considered the Lakota to be allies but the Shoshone were enemies. He had made a sort of peace with Many Lives and his band of Shoshone many years ago, but they were the exception.

But now, there were no more Shoshone, no Cheyenne and no Lakota. Except for those confined to reservations. As Joe rode along, he felt more than ever like he was the last survivor of a time gone by.

He caught sight of a deer about a thousand feet away. Looked like he wasn't as alone as he thought. The wind was blowing from the deer toward Joe, so the deer couldn't catch his scent. Its head was down and it was grazing.

Joe pulled his Winchester and jacked a round into the chamber.

He turned his horse toward the deer and started forward at a walk. He wanted to get as close as he could for the shot. He wasn't like his brother, able to make impossible shots that people would talk about long afterward.

As he got closer, he saw there were two more. All three were does. Not an animal a hunter would brag about shooting, but Joe wasn't looking for a trophy. He was looking for supper.

With the wind blowing toward him, sound wouldn't carry well to the deer. The ground was soft and there were no sticks to crack under a hoof, so the deer didn't hear Joe advancing. Even still, when he was three hundred feet away, he felt he was close enough. If he got too close, the deer would hear him regardless of the wind. A deer can burst into a run and cover a mile in a mighty short time.

He brought the rifle to his shoulder. His left shoulder, with his left hand in place to work the trigger. He didn't have to be Johnny to make this shot. He sighted in on a spot just beyond the shoulder of the closest deer and pulled the trigger.

Two of the does burst into a run. But the one he had aimed at was lying in the grass.

There was a stand of pine a mile away, which was where Joe made his camp for the night. He cut a spit and began roasting a deer steak, and he put a kettle of coffee on.

That night, with the fire burning to keep wolves away, he stretched out in his blankets and looked up at the stars. They seemed so big.

Years earlier, he would have been cautious about having a fire. A flame can be seen for miles. He would have at the very least dug a fire pit, which can cut down on a fire's visibility. But he figured anyone he would have been trying to avoid were long gone.

The following morning, with his belly full of venison, he sat in the saddle on a small grassy hill and watched a train chugging along in the distance. Clouds of white smoke puffed from the smoke stack.

"You don't belong out here," Joe said. As though the train could hear him.

He thought of his last visit with Matt and Peddie at their cabin outside the valley.

Matt's hair was now steel gray, and his face had lines carved into it. But he was still the same old Matt. Filled with philosophy and ten-dollar words.

"Change is inevitable," Matt said, as they sat at the table. Peddie had fried up a durned good ribeye. "It's a part of life. Just like with the seasons. One summer is not like the one before it."

Joe said, "Don't mean I have to like it."

Matt laughed, and then so did Joe. Matt, a man who could embrace the changing winds and find something good in them, and Joe, a man of the past.

Years ago, Matt had pulled a ten-dollar word out of his hat when he was talking about Johnny. *Morose.* As Joe sat in the saddle and watched the train grow smaller in the distance, he wondered if he had allowed himself to grow morose over the years.

4

Two days later, Joe was in the Bighorn Mountains. He was riding along a slope that was covered with a deep pine forest. About ten miles to the northeast was the Little Bighorn River, where the Army colonel George Custer had lost his life in a foolhardy attack on a band of Lakota many times the size of the cavalry outfit he was leading. The newspapers were making Custer out to be a hero and were already calling the battle Custer's Last Stand. But from what Joe could see, Custer got what he asked for.

That battle had been eight years earlier, and though the Lakota had won, it had been the beginning of the end for them.

Joe rode along, following a slope that leveled out at one point. The trees stood tall, and he had a view of the slope beyond, and another further away. Between the ridge he was on and the next one was an open, rocky expanse that was essentially a wide pass. The shelf was facing to the south and a little east, which meant the shelf faced away from most of the storms.

Might be a good place to stay for a while, he thought. Maybe spend the winter. He would build a lean-to for the summer months, then something a little stronger for when the weather grew colder.

He built a campfire that night, and roasted the remainder of his venison. Then he sat by the fire with a tin cup filled with coffee.

His horse was picketed a short distance from the fire. Joe said, "Horse, I think we'll live here a while."

Come morning, Joe grabbed the axe and went to work cutting some pine poles. He tied them to two trunks of two ponderosa pines that grew about eight feet apart. Then he created a thatched roof of pine boughs. When he was done, he had a lean-to that was large enough for him and his gear.

He went about making a wider one, nearby, with two pine poles tied to trees and a third one in the middle, all held together with a ladder-like framework of pine poles, and he thatched it with boughs. Now the horse would have a workable stable.

He sat by the fire that night, and thought about his supplies. The coffee wouldn't last forever. He might also need some additional blankets. You can never have too many blankets for a winter in these mountains.

He would also need a saw and a shovel, maybe some more rope, and some cans of beans. Fresh meat was hard to come by in the winter.

He had worked on and off at the Circle M for the past few years, earning money when needed, and he had a little cash, but not much.

He had heard of a little town called Paintrock that was starting up a few miles south of the Bighorns. He could probably get the supplies he needed there, but he would need more cash.

The following day it rained. It was a good test of both lean-tos. Pine bough thatching worked better than some might think, and though there were a couple small drizzles that worked their way through, the thatching held tolerably well.

The rain backed off after a time, and Joe sat by the fire with mist in the air around him. The sky was covered with clouds, and there was no visible sunset. The land simply darkened as night came on.

Joe thought of Kate. He wondered if she would have been able to live a life in the mountains with him, if she hadn't been committed to marrying Elias Compton. After all, she was a civilized woman. She had grown up in England, with a roof over her head and a soft bed to sleep in. Joe wondered if he could ever have made a life with her. He wondered if she could have been happy in a cabin in the mountains, any more than he could have been happy living in a house and tilling the land.

He supposed they were two people who shared a moment in time, but whose lives were on vastly different paths.

The following morning, he opened a can of beans. Then he saddled up and rode through the mountains, to hunt up some supper. As he was riding along, he found the source of the cash he would need for winter supplies. A trail of unshod hooves cutting through a small ravine between ridges, tearing up the grass and the dirt. Wild horses. He counted seven of them.

Mustanging is not easy for a man by himself, but he didn't need to catch many. Four or five should be enough to get him enough cash for his winter supplies. A couple of cattle ranches had started up in the basin between the Big Horns and the Absarokas further to the west, and they would need horses. Joe had never seen a ranch that didn't need horses.

The ravine had a lot of grass but also a scattering of alders and oaks. He thought it would make a good place for a makeshift corral. That afternoon, he cut poles and built a corral in the small ravine. It was rugged work but he was a strong man, and he was in no hurry. A shovel would have been handy so he could set posts for the corral, but instead he built a corral that was made of rope in some areas and pine poles tied to trees in others.

By the time his work was done the sun was trailing low. He stepped back to look at what he had built.

"Ain't purty," he said, "but it'll do."

The following morning, as soon as the sky began to lighten, he was saddling up. He wanted to get an early start trailing them mustangs. He left his buckskin shirt at his camp, and was in a range shirt and vest. He had a lariat looped over his saddle horn, and a length of rope coiled and tied to his saddle.

He caught up with the mustangs about mid-morning. They were in a grassy meadow, the Big Horns standing tall in the distance beyond. The horses were grazing like they didn't have a care in the world.

Joe took the lariat in one hand. He had learned to use a lariat with his left hand. He couldn't throw a loop as well as he had with his right, but he was good enough to get the job done.

Time to go to work.

5

Five days later, Joe rode along a flat, grassy stretch west of the mountains, and behind him was a line of four mustangs. He now carried his scattergun tied to his back with a length of rawhide. Should he need it, he could grab the gun and pull it around.

Ahead of him was a ranch. The house was two floors tall, with white clapboards and a small front porch. At the center of the roof were three chimneys. Near the house stood a barn, and a little ways beyond was a long cabin built of logs. Probably the bunkhouse, Joe figured.

A man was walking toward him from the barn. He was maybe thirty, with a long, loping stride. He looked to Joe like a man who logged a lot of hours on the back of a horse. The man was in tan canvas pants and a red shirt, and a gray Boss of the Plains hat was pulled down over his temples

Joe said, "I'm looking for Henry Lovell."

"Ain't here," the man said. "I'm Ike Jenkins, his ramrod. You looking to sell them ponies?"

"That I am. My name's Joe McCabe."

Joe reached down to shake the man's hand.

Jenkins said, "McCabe, huh? That's a name that's mentioned from time to time around here."

"That would be my brother they're talking about. He can't seem to keep himself out of situations that make folks want to talk about him."

"Them horses broke?"

Joe shook his head. "I'm not a hand at breaking 'em. That was always my brother Matt's specialty."

They dickered about a price for a few minutes, and Joe settled for a little less than he figured Josh would have offered, but it was good enough.

With cash rolled up and tucked into his vest pocket, Joe rode back to his camp in the mountains.

As the summer passed, he rethatched the roof of the two lean-tos. Pine boughs can grow brown and begin to shrivel after a time, and then they don't stop the rain as well.

He shot deer for supper and began drying some of the venison to make jerky. He ate raspberries and blackberries that grew wild on the mountain slopes, and in more open areas he found roots he could dig.

One morning he sat in the saddle while a mountain lion walked along about five hundred feet further up the slope. Joe held his rifle in his hands.

Joe said, "Just keep walkin' along, kitty-cat. I don't want no trouble."

The cat apparently didn't either. It disappeared into some trees, and then Joe continued riding along.

He tanned some deer hide to make buckskin pants and new moccasins, and he cut some into rawhide strips to sew together and make snowshoes.

One night he was chewing on some venison when his horse gave a nervous nicker, and Joe saw two eyes glowing in the darkness. He knew enough about wild animals to know he was looking at the eyes of a wolf.

Odd that a wolf would come this near the fire, he thought. He grabbed his scattergun.

The critter came forward. It was indeed a wolf. It was gray, and bigger than any German Shepherd Joe had ever seen.

It stood its ground at the edge of the firelight and stared at him. It wasn't growling, and its back fur wasn't standing up. It seemed to be alone.

Might be hungry, Joe thought. He tossed a chunk of venison toward the wolf. It skittered back a few steps as the meat landed in the dirt. Then it approached the meat cautiously, sniffing at it but keeping its eyes on Joe.

"Careful," Joe said. "It's hot."

The wolf grabbed the meat in its teeth and then trotted back into the darkness.

Joe cut off another piece of venison for himself, but he kept his scattergun within reach just in case the wolf hadn't gone far. Though he had fed the animal, it could still be dangerous. *A wild animal can be unpredictable*, Joe thought. *Like a human.*

After a few minutes, the wolf was back. It stood at the edge of the firelight, like it had before.

Joe could see it was a male. He said, "Back for more, boy?"

Joe cut the wolf a piece of meat and tossed it to him. This time the wolf didn't back off as the meat flew through the air. It landed and the wolf began chewing on it where it landed.

Then the wolf slipped away into the darkness.

Joe built up the fire and then crawled into the lean-to and into his roll of blankets. The open end of the lean-to was only a few yards from the fire. Joe could feel the warmth of the flames, and the closed end of the lean-to would trap some of the heat. Even though it was summer, nights in the mountains could be a little chilly.

When the eastern sky was lightening to a steel gray, Joe climbed out of his blankets. He always seemed to wake up about an hour before full daybreak. He grabbed his scattergun and stepped outside the lean-to.

The fire was just a smoldering reminder of what it had been the night before. And at the edge of the camp was the wolf, curled up.

In the early morning light, Joe could clearly see that it was a gray wolf. What some folks called a timber wolf. It looked at Joe with sleepy eyes and then got to its feet.

Joe got some tinder and set it on top of the smoldering, blackened wood of the campfire, and placed an armful of sticks on top of the tinder. He then began fanning at the fire with his hat. Joe and the wolf were watching each other warily.

Glowing embers beneath the tinder came to life, and little flames fluttered through the tinder and then caught onto the larger sticks. Joe took some larger pieces he had cut from a deadfall and set them into the fire.

Joe's horse seemed calm. Apparently the wolf had been there most of the night and the horse had gotten used to him.

"What's going on with you?" Joe said to the wolf.

Of course, Joe didn't really expect the animal to answer. But when you lived alone long enough, you started talking to the animals in your life. Some did even when they weren't alone. Aunt Ginny had taken in a stray cat in Jubilee, and she talked to it. She said the animals can catch your tone of voice and some can even feel your emotions somehow. That went along with talk he had heard from a Cheyenne shaman once.

Joe noticed some beads around the wolf's neck. Looked like they were strung together with rawhide. Joe wasn't quite sure which tribe they signified, but he didn't think it was Cheyenne.

More than one Indian tribe tamed wolves and used them as watch dogs or beasts of burden. Some even bred wolves. If this wolf had belonged to some Indians, it might explain why he was so comfortable around a campfire.

Joe said, "So, what happened to you, boy?"

The wolf looked at him, his ears perked.

Joe said, "Did your master go and get himself killed? Or did he run you off a reservation before some skittish soldier killed you for being a wolf."

The wolf looked hungry and Joe was too. Joe

opened a can of beans and began heating them on the fire. If the wolf wanted meat, he was going to have to wait for Joe to do some hunting.

Joe said, "Well, if you're gonna hang around here and eat my food, I should prob'ly give you a name. The Cheyenne word for gray is Ee-poh-oh. Actually, it means *it's gray*, but close enough. Maybe I can call you Poe, for short. You like that?"

The wolf looked at him.

Joe said, "You may not be Cheyenne, but if you spend enough time around me, you will be."

For the next week, Joe hunted the pine forest of the slope where he had his camp and the next slope over, beyond the ravine where he had built his makeshift corral. His goal was to stockpile as much meat as possible for the winter.

He cut some logs and made a small smoking house, so he could smoke venison. At night, he would hang the meat high in a tree. Not only to keep it away from wild animals that might catch the scent, but he didn't want Poe to be tempted.

"I don't think you mean harm," Joe said to him, "but you're a wolf, and you can't change your nature. Any more than a man can."

There were times when he was hunting that Poe would walk alongside the horse, and other times, the wolf would disappear for hours. One time he was gone for two days, and Joe thought he had seen the last of him, but then the wolf came trotting into camp near sunset.

One evening Joe sat by the fire with his long Cheyenne pipe, and Poe was curled up on the ground beside him with his eyes shut.

Joe said, "In the morning, I'm gonna ride down to town to bring in some supplies. The summer's now mostly gone and we have to start getting ready for the winter. I'm thinking of building a dugout."

He figured when he rode into town, the wolf would disappear. But next morning, as he rode down the slope, his bedroll and saddlebags tied to the back of his saddle, Poe trotted along beside him.

Joe headed for Paintrock. Not that he had been there before. From what he heard, it was a new town, not more than a couple of years old.

The last time he had ridden through this area, there had been no towns at all, and no ranches. But that had been years ago.

Joe didn't know exactly where Paintrock was and he had no map, but he had asked the ramrod at the Lovell Ranch for directions. Joe followed those directions, riding west until the Big Horns were behind him and he found himself in open grasslands, and then turned south.

The grass had been springtime green when he wandered into these mountains weeks earlier, but now it was brown.

The land was sometimes flat, and sometimes rose into steep hills. All the time, Poe was trotting along beside him.

Joe wondered what civilized folk like Aunt Ginny would think of the sight of Joe riding along with a wolf beside him.

He doubted the sight would shake Bree or Em. He had seen some among the Cheyenne who had a natural way with animals, but Bree and Em were two of the few he had seen among white folks.

Joe saw tendrils of smoke rising in the distance ahead, and figured he had found Paintrock. It was mid-afternoon. He planned to stock up on supplies and make camp outside of town, and in the morning he would head back to the mountains.

He rode for another mile, and then he saw ahead of him a line of buildings. They looked like crude shacks. Maybe eight or ten of them. What often passed for a frontier town.

"I suppose this is where we should part company," Joe said to the wolf. "I doubt folks down there would take kindly to you."

Poe trotted along beside Joe for a while further, then stopped and watched Joe ride on. After a couple of hundred feet, Joe looked over his shoulder and the wolf was no longer in sight. Must have run off. Joe realized he was going to miss the critter.

He found a general store in town and stocked up on flour, coffee, and lots of cans of beans. He also bought blankets, and like he had planned, a shovel and a buck saw.

He didn't normally travel with a pack horse, but decided to make an exception. The man who ran the livery sold him a mule for five dollars and his Colt revolver in trade. Joe hardly used the pistol, anyway.

Once the mule was loaded up with supplies, Joe found he had thirty cents left, so he went to the saloon for a bottle of beer. The place had an uneven roofline and an earthen floor. Probably had been built in one afternoon. It was hardly the Second Chance, but Joe hadn't had a taste of beer in a while.

The bar was like many he had seen in frontier saloons—a couple of crudely cut planks balanced across wooden crates. He stood and drank a warm beer.

With the afternoon shadows stretching long, Joe rode out of town. He found a stand of alders near a small creek and made his camp for the night. One alder had fallen and the wood was reasonably seasoned, so he used the saw to cut it up for firewood. The saw teeth were sharp and made short work of the wood.

With the sky growing dark and beans warming in the skillet, Joe sat cross-legged on the ground and lit his pipe. The horse and mule were picketed nearby.

The sky grew dark and Joe drew smoke from his pipe, and allowed the peace of the night to settle on him.

After a time, the mule started acting panicky, so Joe got to his feet and, taking the mule by the hackamore, he began to stroke his nose.

"What's wrong, boy?"

The horse seemed calm, but the mule looked like he wanted to bolt.

Then Joe saw the glowing eyes at the edge of the camp, and he couldn't help but smile.

He said, "Poe. I thought I'd seen the last of you."

The wolf walked into camp, and Joe dug into his shirt and pulled out a strip of jerky. He held it out, and the wolf came over and took it from his hand.

Joe sat back down by the fire, and the wolf sat with him. The mule calmed down, and Joe handed the wolf another strip of jerky.

From somewhere off in the darkness, another wolf howled. Poe raised his face to the night sky and returned the call.

Joe grinned. "Give 'em one for me, too."

Poe raised his head and howled again.

6

Joe sometimes hunted close to the camp, and when he did, he was on foot. Other times he took his horse, and he ranged as far as a few miles.

He came to know where the game trails were, and he would sometimes find a concealed spot along one. A thick bushy pine was ideal. And he would wait for sometimes an hour or two. He would picket the horse off a ways, in a location that the wind was blowing towards, so any deer approaching along the game trail wouldn't catch the scent.

He didn't use the same game trail every day. You shoot a couple of deer along one game trail, and the animals will alter their route.

Deer tend to bed down in a meadow or grassy area at night, then travel throughout the day in a roughly circular route, searching for food and finding water, and end their wanderings where they began so they could bed down again for the night. They didn't always follow the exact same route, but it was often close.

Joe learned the movements of the deer. Which meadows they were using at night. Which time of day they tended to arrive at certain watering holes or springs or streams.

One day he was riding along the side of a ridge. He was near the crest, and the trees were few and scattered at this altitude. Sections of bedrock were exposed, creating what looked like blobs of misshapen rock. Juniper bushes were here and there.

Joe had been thinking about making some deer stew. He was in search of roots and wild onions he had known a Cheyenne woman to put in deer stew, years ago.

He saw what he wanted, and swung out of the saddle. A patch of wild onions, growing tall and green. He had his Winchester in one hand and he left his horse's rein trailing. He had left the scattergun back at camp because he didn't think he would be needing it in these hills. A scattergun was more of a close-range weapon.

He knelt and pulled an onion. The bulb had a smell of earth and sweet onion. Joe wasn't one to bite into an onion, but he sure loved what they did to a stew.

Suddenly, the horse gave a loud warning snort and then pulled back. Joe, still on one knee and with the onion in one hand, looked over his shoulder at the horse. "What's ailin' you?"

The horse turned and charged off. That was when the bear stepped around a large section of bedrock, not twenty feet from him. A large grizzly, with brown fur that took on a silver shine in the sunlight.

Joe blinked with surprise. *Getting careless in my old age*, he thought.

He said, "Move on along, big feller. Don't want no trouble with you."

But the bear rose on its feet and came right at him, moving faster than you would think a bear that size could move. Joe jacked a round into the chamber, but he didn't have time to even bring the rifle to his shoulder. He fired from the hip and saw a section of fur fly from the bear's midsection, and then the bear was on top of him.

The rifle got knocked away, and the bear threw Joe to the ground. The bear clawed at him with its right front paw, and Joe raised his left forearm to catch the force of the blow. Part of his buckskin sleeve below the elbow was torn away. The bear then sunk its teeth into his arm.

Joe reached around with his right hand to his left side, and pulled his long knife. Since he didn't have much grip strength with that hand, he palmed the end of the hilt and pushed the blade into the bear's neck, as far as it could go. A desperate last move, he knew. If the blade didn't stop the bear, then Joe would soon be dead.

The bear swiped at him with his other paw, and Joe caught it in the face. The bear then pulled away.

Joe got to his hands and knees and tried to scramble away, his left hand and forearm smeared with blood. The bear was back up on its hind feet, swinging its head back and forth. Joe could see the handle of the knife sticking out of the bear's neck, but he couldn't tell how deep the blade was or if it had even hit a vital spot. So much of a grizzly is muscle and fat.

Joe tried to get to his feet. He was at the edge of a small shelf, and the gravel gave way beneath him, and he went tumbling.

He rolled and bounced, and came to a crashing stop

at the trunk of a pine.

He figured he might have been unconscious for a short while—he wasn't sure. He looked up the hill and saw that he had fallen nearly fifty feet down the slope. It was steep, and he didn't think he could climb back up.

He was bleeding from the bite on his arm, and his beard was soaked with blood from his face. His left knee felt numb and he thought he might have hurt it on the way down the slope.

He had twisted a knee quite bad in Texas, years ago, and then again in California. He remembered it feeling about the way it did now.

The bear wasn't in sight, but that didn't mean it wasn't nearby.

He got to his feet, reaching out with his right hand to the tree trunk to steady himself. Then he started down the slope, hobbling and stumbling along. Reaching out to tree trunks. More than once he went down on all fours.

His camp was maybe a half mile down and to his left. Not far by horseback, but it sure seemed a long way on foot and with a bad knee.

He stopped and looked over his shoulder. He saw nothing back there, and even more important, he heard nothing. He didn't think the bear was following him.

Blood was coming out of his forearm in a steady trickle. Out here in the wilderness, he couldn't afford to be weakened by blood loss. With his right hand, he unbuckled the belt that he wore outside his buckskin shirt. He slid off the now-empty sheath and let if fall to the pine needles at his feet. Then he wrapped it around his left forearm above the gash and pulled the belt tight, cutting off the supply of blood. He pulled it tight until he felt his fingers tingle.

He was concerned about his face, too. The bear's claws had dug deep, and he could see the blood now dripping to the front of his buckskin shirt.

He held the belt tight with his teeth, and then knelt down and dug with the fingers of his right hand through the pine needles and to the earth beneath.

The ground was damp, so he dug out a fistful of it and rubbed it into the cuts on his face. He thought there were three cuts. One on his chin that wasn't bad, but one by his mouth and one on his cheekbone were bleeding bad. He pushed dirt into them, to block the flow of blood.

Then he continued on.

It was near dark when he came stumbling into his camp. He had two canteens. One was on his saddle—his horse was probably miles away by now—and the other was in his lean-to. With water from the canteen, he washed out the bite on his arm and the deep scratches on his face. Then he drank what was left of it. An old Cheyenne shaman had told him once that when you've lost some blood, you need to get water back into you.

He knew what his next step was, and he dreaded it. It was gonna hurt like the dickens. His saddle bags were in the lean-to, and he dug into them to find a small tin pint container of moonshine.

Johnny said once that he had learned during his time with the Rangers that this was one sure-fire way of keeping away infection. Granny Tate had said she saw it work, more than once.

Joe wouldn't let himself cry out, as he dumped moonshine into the gash on his arm. Too much pride for that. But he grit his teeth tight and tears streamed down his face.

Now for his face itself. He had packed in mud earlier, but now he had to wash all of it out and let the alcohol soak into the wounds. He had no mirror, but he did the best he could, holding his face to the sky and dumping in the moonshine.

The liquid ran down over his cheeks and to his neck. Smelled awful. He had never taken to hard liquor. But he could tell by how much it hurt that it was finding the right spots.

He didn't have a needle and thread. He thought maybe he would remedy that the next time he went for supplies. He wrapped a soft patch of doeskin around his forearm, and tied it at both ends. Hold the skin together and keep dirt out.

It was getting dark, but he was too exhausted to even bother with a fire. He climbed into his blankets and as soon as his head hit the rolled-up blanket he used for a pillow, he was asleep.

When he woke up, it was dark, and he was thirsty as all get-out. He crawled out of the lean-to, being careful because of his forearm and his knee.

He found Poe at the front of the lean-to, lying down but holding his head up.

"Poe," Joe said.

He realized the wolf was standing guard. Poe had been gone all day, but he must have come back and found Joe asleep and wounded.

Joe scratched the wolf's head. Joe said, "Poe, you are truly a wonder."

The wolf wagged his tail a couple of times.

Joe thought again about how thirsty he was. There was a small creek a five-minute walk away. Five minutes under normal circumstances. But tonight it seemed an impossible distance.

Then he heard the sound of a hoof shifting on the ground. He looked over to where the sound had come from and saw his horse was there. The horse had apparently found his way back to camp.

Joe limped his way over and took the canteen from the saddle, and he drank deep.

Using one hand, he unsaddled the horse and then slid the saddle away. Then he went back to his lean-to. He scratched Poe's head again and said, "Danged, if you don't beat all."

7

Come morning, Joe used the axe to cut himself a stick he could use as a cane. His knee didn't seem to be swollen like it had been back in Texas and California, but it hurt bad enough and he knew it would probably be a few days before he could put full weight on it.

He didn't feel like he had a fever, which meant there probably wasn't any infection. Wounds as deep as his were, there would probably be a fever if there was infection. He was glad there wasn't. He didn't relish the thought of washing the wounds out with moonshine again.

Gonna need water, he thought. He took both canteens, and using his cane, he hobbled to the little creek. The five-minute-walk took him nearly fifteen minutes.

Once he was back at camp, he started a fire going. A haunch of venison was up in a tree where he had tied it the day before, but lowering it seemed like too much work now. So instead he opened a can of beans and dumped them into the skillet, and he started some coffee heating.

Poe was still there.

Joe said, "Wolf, we're in bad shape. I done lost both my rifle and my knife. All we got left is my scattergun, but it ain't much use for hunting."

Joe knew what he had to do. He wouldn't survive long in the wild with no weapons. He had to go back up the ridge and find his rifle. He figured his knife was long gone, because it was stuck in the bear and the bear was probably miles away.

He had another knife, the smaller fold-up knife he kept in the pocket of his buckskin shirt. It would have to suffice for now.

He didn't want to saddle the horse. His knee still couldn't hold much weight, and now he had bruises all over his back from his tumble down the hill. He hadn't felt the bruises so much the day before, but he did when he woke up. He knew he couldn't get back there on foot, so he gritted his teeth against the pain, balanced himself on his good leg, and hefted the saddle to the horse's back.

Once the horse was ready, he then had to face getting into the saddle even though his left leg could hardly hold any weight.

Joe figured he would give it a try, anyway. He got his left foot into the stirrup and tried to step up and swing onto the saddle, but he couldn't get off the ground.

Poe was sitting and looking at him, his ears perked and his head cocked a little.

Joe said, "What're you looking at?"

Joe led the horse to a short pine out beyond the camp. He stepped onto one of the low branches, the branch bowing under his weight, and then from the tree he climbed up and onto the back of the horse. Weren't pretty, but at least he was in the saddle.

He rode the horse up the ridge, toward where he had seen the bear.

The Winchester was where he had hoped it would be, at the top of the slope he had tumbled down. He was concerned it might have gotten broken in the fight with the bear, but it looked intact.

He climbed down from the horse. The rifle was a little damp from having been outdoors all night. Cartridges were not water-tight, so he worked the action and the cartridges jumped out of the gun. He dug into his vest pocket for twelve dry ones and reloaded the rifle.

He led the horse to a section of bedrock that was about two feet high, and used it like he had the small pine to climb back into the saddle. It was a little more difficult with the rifle in one hand.

The wolf was still with him. Joe looked down at him and said, "Danged bear run off with my knife."

Joe noticed a bird circling in the sky up ahead. Looked like a crow. He nudged the horse ahead, and saw the crow swoop down to a point just beyond his sight, but down the ridge a little ways. Joe decided to check it out.

He found the grizzly in the grass between two tall pines. The bear wasn't moving, and three crows were chewing on it.

Joe shooed the birds off, and he pulled his long knife from the bear's neck.

Joe said to the wolf, "You're gonna get a treat. Bear meat, for a change. And you know what? I'm gonna have a nice warm bearskin blanket for the winter."

8

Joe worked on the bearskin, scraping away fat. It was pinned down to the ground with wooden pegs and was stretched to its full length. Joe had seen Cheyenne women use a specialized tool for scraping the skin, but he used his knife.

A bearskin robe or blanket could keep you mighty warm in the winter. He had one years ago when he was living with the Cheyenne. Danged hard way to go about getting one this time, though.

There was a natural spring about a half mile from his camp, where water trickled out through a crack in some bedrock and filled a small pool. Much bigger than the small creek that was near his camp. Joe had been climbing in once in a while, because he didn't want to get too foul-smelling. He had no soap, but the water was rich in minerals and did a tolerable job.

He always made sure to fill his canteen from where the water came from the rocks. He didn't want to drink from where he had been washing.

Two days after the bear attack, he went to the spring to wash out the scratches on his face and the bite on his forearm.

He looked at his reflection in the water. One scratch was on his chin, and mostly covered by his beard, but there was a deep one along his cheekbone, and another one near his brow. Two pronounced red stripes.

He said, "You done got yourself lookin' mighty hideous."

He worked at smoking bear meat, adding to his stash of smoked deer meat. He tied it to a rope and suspended it from a pine branch twenty feet off the ground. It would keep nighttime critters away from it. Come winter, the meat would freeze, which would help preserve it even more.

At night, he sat by the fire, making a bear claw necklace. At times, he would just sit and look at the night, or look toward the fire. Never into it. He would often smoke his pipe, and sometimes Poe was at his side. Joe would reach over and stroke the wolf's head or the back of his neck.

After a week, his knee felt stronger, and he decided to get to work building his dugout cabin.

A couple of hundred feet back from where Joe had built his lean-tos was an earthen embankment. Grass grew over it so the embankment held together when it rained. Joe decided this was where he would build his dugout.

To build a dugout cabin, you have to dig, so he went to work with his new shovel. All he needed was one room. It didn't even have to be tall enough for him to stand up in. It just needed to be big enough for him to sleep in, and to stow his gear.

He cut pine logs and pushed them into place to serve as timbers—to hold the roof of the dugout up so it wouldn't fall in on him. He had brought a hammer and some nails with him from Montana, and he used them to nail together the framework.

Once the dugout was deep enough and the framework in place, he went to work cutting more logs, and fitted them over the opening of the dugout.

He worked throughout what was left of the summer. Most of the days he worked on the dugout, but some days he hunted. He smoked as much meat as he could, and he made pounds of jerky.

All this time, Poe stayed with him. The wolf continued his habit of running off once in a while, and was gone overnight a couple of times. But he always came back.

Joe ate only what he hunted, or whatever berries he could find or roots he could dig. He wanted to hold his stash of canned food for the winter.

He knew the snow could be deep in these mountains, so he continued the work he had started on a pair of snowshoes. If the winter was long and his food supply got too thin, he would have to venture out into the snow and do some hunting.

The nights began to grow colder, and soon a stand of oak down below the ridge was coming alive with autumn red.

He increased the pace of his work, putting the finishing touches on his little dugout cabin. He built the front wall out of logs, and he hauled rocks to the cabin and built a chimney at one end of the wall, and a small opening in the chimney that would serve as a hearth. He used mud as mortar. The hearth wasn't big, but it wouldn't take much of a fire to keep the little dugout warm.

He nailed a wool blanket into place over a small opening at one end. The opening was large enough for him to crawl through.

He cut logs and chinked them together to make a small stable for the horse and mule, and made a roof that sloped downward. It would keep the cold wind out, and their body heat would keep the interior above freezing.

One night, as Joe was sitting by his campfire, the night air cold enough that he could see his breath, he heard a wolf howl from out in the darkness. Then another.

Poe was stretched out on the ground by the fire, but he lifted his head. A third wolf howled, this one closer.

Poe looked at Joe, then got to his feet. Poe trotted to the edge of the firelight, then looked back at Joe.

Joe said, "Go ahead."

The wolf ran off into the darkness. *Every now and then, a critter needs to run with his own kind,* Joe figured.

The night grew colder, and the stars overhead were gone, meaning there was a cloud cover. Joe could smell snow on the air.

City folks think it's only a myth that you can smell snow, but anyone who has lived in the mountains knows you can. Joe figured it was time to try the dugout.

He loaded his gear into the cabin, then built a small

fire in the hearth. The dugout was rich in the smell of earth and soon in the smell of wood smoke. Two smells Joe loved. He wrapped up in his blankets, keeping his rifle and knife within reach, and drifted off to sleep.

He was awakened by the sound of a dog whining outside. Joe lifted the blanket and found it was too dark to see anything out there, but he knew who the animal had to be.

He said, "Come on in."

Poe climbed in through the opening. His back and neck were covered with snow.

"You big baby," Joe said.

Joe had made the cabin big enough for the two of them, and Poe plopped down by the fire. Joe set some more sticks into the hearth, then crawled back into his blankets.

Come morning, Joe and the wolf stepped outside and found about six inches of snow on the ground. Joe scraped it away from the spot where he built his campfires, and as soon as a fire was going, he put on a kettle of coffee to boil.

He could have made coffee in the cabin, but he preferred being outdoors as much as possible.

Once the coffee was ready, he filled a tin cup and walked to the edge of the shelf. He looked down at the ridge below and the one beyond. Snow covered the land. Pine boughs were weighted down with it. The air was cold and crisp, and the sky a clear, early-winter blue.

Joe was lonely at times, and probably always would be, he figured, because of the life he led. But mornings like this, he felt he wouldn't trade his life for any other.

9

Winter came on strong. One morning Joe had to climb through a foot of snow to get out of his little cabin.

There was more than one day when it was so cold outside he left his cabin only to relieve himself or to scoop snow to boil for coffee water. Otherwise, he remained inside, wrapped in his bearskin blanket, with the fire burning.

One day he decided to take a walk around. The weather had warmed up a little. He figured the temperature to be around thirty degrees.

There was about three feet of snow on the ground, though it varied. In some areas, the wind had blown enough of it away so what remained was only a few inches deep. In other areas it drifted to five or six feet.

Joe tied on his snow shoes, and with his rifle in hand, he started out. Poe went with him, running through the snow in leaps and bounds.

Joe had cut a hole through a wool blanket, and with the hole in the blanket pulled down over his head, it served as a heavy pancho. With his buckskin shirt under it, the buckskin pants he had made, and his felt hat pulled down almost to his ears, he was warm enough.

The snow was light and fluffy because there hadn't been a day above freezing. A man could easily sink to his knees in snow like this, but with his snowshoes on, he found the walking easy. He would still sink a few inches into the snow, and the snow would pile up onto his snowshoes, so every so often he had to stop and shake the snow free.

Further along the ridge, he came to an open area that he knew to be rocky, but the rocks were under the cover of snow. Joe stood and looked at the area. It was gleaming white in the sunshine.

Poe was about to run out there, but Joe said, "Hold on, mutt. Stay here with me. Nothing might happen, but you stay with me. Just in case."

Then Joe saw it begin—what he was concerned might happen. First some snow at the top of the open stretch began to move. Then more began to slide downward.

"Get back!" Joe called.

He shuffled back in his snowshoes until he was behind the trunk of a pine. The wolf was close up beside him.

The snow slide picked up speed, a cloud of snow rising above it. The slide went roaring down the side of the ridge, and Joe felt the ground shake.

And then it was over, and all became silent. Some pines at the bottom of the slide had been uprooted, but the snow around the tree Joe had positioned himself behind was holding tight.

A snow slide was a beautiful sight, Joe thought, but deadly to be caught in. The cloud of snow was still overhead, the snow drifting down like tiny, icy rain.

The months wore on. Joe took hikes to the top of the ridge, where the air was a cold, wintertime clean. The kind of air you can find only in the mountains in winter.

As harsh as winter can be up here, it was his favorite time of year in the mountains.

More snow fell, and then was followed by some warm days. Snow would melt a bit, and then freeze at night to form an icy crust.

Joe ate from his supply of canned food and smoked meat. One time he went out on snow shoes and saw a deer shoulder deep in the snow. He used his rifle, and he and Poe had fresh meat that night.

Eventually, the mountains came to life with spring. Stream beds that had been dry in late summer were now running strong with cold water. Soon the snow was gone, except for the highest reaches of the Big Horns. Joe started building his fires outdoors again.

The ground was still too cold and wet to sit on, so Joe hauled a fallen log over to the fire. He was sitting on the log one night, his long pipe in one hand and the fire crackling away.

He started thinking thoughts that he had applied to Poe at one time. Every critter needs to run with his own kind, every so often. He found himself hankering for a beer, and to hear the sound of conversation around him. The sound of laughter, and the tinkling of a piano.

The saloon in Paintrock was a little small. He thought he might head further south. Maybe to Cheyenne. He would need some more money, which brought the Lovell Ranch to mind again. Maybe when the weather was warmer, he would do some more mustanging, and then take a ride south.

PART TWO

The Fugitives

10

May, 1884

Joe was in his range shirt and his old leather vest. His scattergun was now in a deerskin sheath that was slung over his back.

He reined up in front of a saloon, the name TRAIN WHISTLE on a sign above the door. Joe had his mule with him, and he left both the horse and the mule at the hitching rail out front.

It was mid-afternoon. He figured he would have a bottle of beer or two. Maybe enjoy the atmosphere of the saloon for a few hours.

He had delivered seven mustangs to the Lovell Ranch, and got a little better deal on them than he had the first ones. He would buy some supplies before he left town and then head back to the Big Horns.

He wasn't sure he wanted to spend the next winter in the same place. He had never been one to spend too much time in one area. Not since the little Cheyenne gal of long ago. When she chose another warrior over him, he had ridden away. And he seemed to have been riding away ever since. The past few years in Montana had been the longest he had stayed anywhere in a long time.

Maybe he would head to the Absarokas. Or maybe

ride down to Colorado and see if that little valley was still unsettled. The valley where he, Matt and Johnny had wintered, so many years ago. He could always head even further south, and visit Wardtown for a while. Check up on Tremain and Maddie and the others.

He was in no hurry to decide. It was still late spring.

Joe paid little attention to what day of the week it was. In the mountains, the white-man calendar had little relevance. But he figured it was a Wednesday. Or Thursday. He hadn't expected the saloon to be busy, and it wasn't. A couple of cowhands were sitting at a table in the corner. They looked bored. One was absently shuffling a deck of cards.

A woman who worked there was sitting at a table, and she looked bored, too. She was probably about Bree's age, Joe figured, but it was hard to tell because of the grease paint on her face.

She gave him a look like she saw a potential customer, but then decided against it. Joe figured he looked too wild.

His hair was longer than ever, falling a few inches past his shoulders, and his beard reached to the center of his chest. The grizzly scars on his face didn't help any.

A saloon woman wasn't his game, anyway. He admitted to himself that he had tried saloon women a couple of times years ago, to see if it would help him get away from the loneliness that dogged him. Especially after Kate. But it didn't, so he decided there were better ways to spend his money.

He bellied-up to the bar and leaned his rifle against it. The boys at the table each had a mug of beer in front of them, but Joe was a little leery of beer from a tap. He had seen it go bad too often.

"What'll you have?" the bartender said.

He looked to be pushing fifty, with white hair and a thick mustache.

Joe said, "A bottle of beer will do."

Joe decided to set the rifle on the bar. Keep it within easier reach. Not that there looked to be any real threat here, he was just being cautious. You live in the wild like Joe preferred, you didn't live long if you weren't cautious.

The bartender said, "Don't see many riflemen, these days. Most men carry a pistol."

"Traded mine away a while back."

"That a scattergun on your back?"

Joe nodded. "Ten gauge."

The bartender set a bottle in front of Joe and pulled the cork. "Budweiser, all the way from Saint Louie."

Joe nodded. Hunter carried the brand, back in Jubilee. Joe took a chug.

The bartender said, "You in town for the hanging?"

Joe hadn't heard about any hanging. He shook his head and said, "Just here for a bottle or two. Buy some supplies. Then I'm headin' out."

The bartender gave him a long look. "You look a little familiar. You been in here before?"

Joe shook his head.

The bartender said, "You kind of remind me of someone. Around the eyes a little. Your name McCabe?"

Joe nodded. "Joe McCabe."

The bartender smiled. "Any relation to *the* McCabes? Johnny McCabe and them?"

Joe nodded. "Johnny's my brother."

"Well, I'll be. I never had the pleasure to meet Johnny himself, but I met his son Jack once, in this very saloon. Must have been five years back. He was standing right where you are, and got himself into a fight with two men. Laid 'em both out on the floor. He came through a couple of years later, with his wife. A pretty young thing. They had been back East. He told me he had been studying for a law degree."

Joe nodded. He had never been much for a lot of talking.

The bartender began to wipe at the bar with a cloth.

He said, "That hanging I mentioned, it's kind of unusual."

"Never been much for watching a hanging."

"They're hanging a woman. Ain't never been a woman hanged in Wyoming Territory, as far as I know."

The bartender was not going to stop talking, so Joe gave a little shrug of resignation. "Who'd she kill?"

"Her husband. Can you imagine that? He and his brother own a gold mine, down outside of Denver. They own part of a mine outside of Jubilee, Montana, too. In fact, if I remember right, that's the place your brother had a ranch at one time."

"Still does."

"The man and his brother also have a cattle ranch in Oregon, and a shipping business. Rolling in money. But then one night his wife just up and slit his throat. Right in bed, while he was sleeping. Can you imagine that?"

Joe said nothing. The bartender clearly found this all intriguing, but Joe didn't. He had seen too much tragedy, too much killing, to find talk of it fascinating.

"Gonna hang her tomorrow," the bartender said. "Katarina Compton, her name is. An English woman. In fact, her husband was, too. And his brother. The whole lot of 'em."

He chuckled. "I suppose if her husband was an Englishman, it would go to figure his brother was, too."

Joe was staring at him. "What'd you say her name was?"

"Katarina Compton. Why, you know the family?"

"Was her maiden name Waddell?"

The bartender shrugged. "Don't rightly know."

"What's her husband's name?"

"Elias Compton. Or it was, before she slit his throat. His brother is Jonah. They say that between the two of them, they own almost half of Oregon. They were expanding their business here. Making a bid on a ranch near Medicine Bow, owned by a judge who died."

Joe stood in silence. Could it be? Was it possible?

He realized he hadn't taken a breath since the bartender gave the woman's name, so he forced himself to draw in some air.

"So," the bartender said, "how do you know the Comptons?"

Joe said nothing, so the bartender left him alone. Joe stood at the bar and finished his beer. He dropped a nickel on the bar and grabbed his rifle.

He said to the bartender, "Which way to the marshal's office?"

"Two blocks down the street."

Joe nodded, and he pushed his way through the swinging doors into the street.

11

Joe left his horse and mule in front of the saloon and headed down the boardwalk on foot. He wasn't like so many cowhands he had seen, like Josh and Dusty, who couldn't go ten feet without saddling up.

He opened the door of the marshal's office and stepped in. One man was pouring a cup of coffee. He was tall with a black mustache, and a badge was pinned to his shirt. Another man was at a desk. Both looked a little startled at Joe. He often got that reaction and was used to it. He looked more like the trappers who roamed the mountains a couple of generations ago than the cowhands of today.

Joe said to the man standing, "You the marshal?"

The man nodded. "That's right."

"You got the lady in here that's due to hang?"

The marshal nodded again.

Joe said, "I need to see her."

The man at the desk said, "Oh you do, do you?"

The marshal said, "The district attorney has left a list of names, and they're the only people allowed to see her. The list is mighty short."

"My name's Joe McCabe and it ain't on any list. But I need to see her."

"Any relation to Jack McCabe?"

Joe nodded. "My nephew. He's a lawyer, nowadays,

up in the town of Jubilee, Montana."

"My name's Jubal Kincaid. I was the marshal here in town when Jack ran afoul of the old outlaw, Victor Falcone."

"He's living up near Jubilee, too. Got hisself a pardon."

Kincaid nodded. "I've heard that, too. I'd like to know the whole story behind it."

"I'd tell you, if I knew. I tend not to ask a lot of questions, and to let people be."

"Not a bad approach." Kincaid took a sip of coffee. "Why do you want to see the prisoner?"

"She'll want to see me if you give her my name."

The other man—Joe figured he was probably a deputy—got to his feet. "It don't matter if the prisoner wants to see you or not. The district attorney left specific instructions. She's got no say in it."

Joe said, "That the way of it?"

Kincaid nodded. "Officially."

"How about unofficially?"

Kincaid paced along the floor for a couple of steps, and took a sip of his coffee.

He said to the deputy, "Go out back and tell her Mister McCabe is here to see her."

The deputy gave a long look at Kincaid.

The marshal said "It wasn't a request."

The deputy had a look on his face that struck Joe as somewhere between disbelief and anger, but he opened a door at the back wall and stepped through. Joe figured the cell block was out back. It was the way of most jails he had seen in towns the size of Cheyenne or Jubilee.

Kincaid said, "You want some coffee?"

Joe shook his head. "Nope. Thanks, anyway."

"Probably for the best. It's not very good. Jailhouse coffee seldom is."

Joe grinned.

The deputy came back. "Her eyes lit up like a kid at Christmas when I gave her your name."

"Go on back," Kincaid said to Joe. "It's against the rules, but why not. She's going to hang tomorrow at noon. I don't see what harm it can do."

The deputy said, "You'll have to leave those guns and that knife with us."

Joe shook his head. "Ain't no man ever taken a weapon from me."

"It'll be all right," Kincaid said. "Go on and see her."

The deputy was giving Kincaid a look that said he thought the marshal was out of his mind.

Joe stopped at the doorway and looked back at Kincaid. "You think she done it? Killed her husband?"

Kincaid shrugged. "That's what the jury decided."

"That ain't what I'm askin'."

"You apparently know the woman. What do you think?"

Joe headed out back.

Kincaid went to his desk and sat down. He took another sip of coffee and set the cup on the desk. It had been a long day and he had a feeling it was going to be a long dark night. It usually was, the night before a hanging. He hoped the man who had just walked into his jail wasn't going to make it harder than it needed to be.

He realized his deputy was staring at him.

Kincaid said, "What is it, Abbott?"

Abbott was about thirty, with neatly combed hair and a normally cleanly shaven face, though at the moment he had stubble. It had been a long day for him, too.

Abbott said, "You let him go back there with those guns and that long knife. We always confiscate weapons before someone visits a prisoner."

"You want to try and take his weapons from him?"

"The district attorney wouldn't like it, if he was to find out."

As tired as he was, Kincaid was starting to get a little riled. "And how is he going to find out?"

Abbot said nothing more.

Kincaid said, "Just because you're the DA's cousin doesn't give you any authority in this office. You got the job because you're his cousin, but that's where the special treatment ends. If you don't like the way I run this office, then set down your badge and walk out."

Abbot shrugged. "I didn't mean anything. I was just wondering, that's all."

Kincaid said, "Taking his weapons wouldn't make him any easier to stop."

"How do you figure that?"

"Partly because of his name, and partly because of the way he carries himself."

Abbott went back to his desk. "I just don't believe all that talk about the McCabes."

"I met Jack McCabe once. Got to talk to him a little. I saw the result of two men who started a fight with him. I met his father once, too. All those stories you hear about them? Most of them are true."

12

Kate had been about Bree's age the last time Joe saw her. He didn't see a whole lot of difference in her now. Her hair was still a light brown color, and was hanging loose and fell in curls down her shoulders. She hadn't gained weight like some women do over the years.

He had known her for only three days, and that had been nigh onto twenty-five years ago. But when her eyes met his, it was like he had seen her just the day before.

There were three cells and she was standing just behind the bars in the one nearest the door. She looked a little rumpled from being in jail, probably in the same dress for days. She looked much like she had twenty-five years ago, when she had been captured by Indians, and Joe and Johnny and Zack Johnson rescued her.

"Joe," she said.

"You ain't changed none," was all he could find to say. Matt would probably have burst into a flowery speech or start reciting some kind of poem, but words never came easy to Joe.

"Yes, I have" she said.

"You're more beautiful than ever."

She was looking at him with a mixture of emotions that only a woman could muster. Joy. Sadness. Wonder. Love.

She said, "I can't believe it's really you. After all

these years."

"Not a day has gone by that I didn't think of you."

"You were in my thoughts, too, every day. I always wondered if you were all right. If you ever found the happiness you so deserved."

She still had the gentle British accent of years ago. It flowed like music.

"I stayed away," Joe said. "I had to."

"In a way, I wish you had now. I hate for you to see me like this."

"You ain't gonna hang. I guarantee it."

"But Joe. You haven't even asked me if I did it. If I killed Elias. That's what they found me guilty of."

"I don't have to."

She reached through the bars to him and he took her hand.

She said, "When I look into your eyes, even after all these years, it's like all of the years that have passed just fall away."

"You sure got a way with words. I hope you know I feel the same way."

"Your face. Those scars."

He noddcd. "Tangled with a grizzly last year."

She couldn't help but smile. "You always did live the most fascinating life."

The other two cells were empty, so they were speaking in private.

He said, "Are they treatin' you all right in here?"

She shrugged her shoulders. "As well as they can, I suppose."

Kincaid stepped in from the office. "I hate to break this up, but if the district attorney catches you in here, I'll be in a whole pile of trouble."

Kate said, "Just a couple of minutes more, Marshal. Please."

Kincaid said, "Two minutes."

He stepped back out.

Kate said, "Joe, I want you to promise me something. Ride out of town. Don't be here tomorrow. As much as I would like to have you at my side for my last day on Earth, I don't want you to see me hang."

"You ain't gonna hang."

"But how can it be prevented? My lawyer lost all of our appeals. There's no more recourse to fall back on."

He nodded. "Yes there is."

"What could it be?"

He grinned. "Me."

13

Joe went to the livery and traded his mule for another horse.

The man who ran the livery was ancient, with a voice that was thin and reedy, and white hair that was wispy and flying every which way.

He said, "I'll throw in that old saddle in the corner, if you'd like. It's been just a-settin' there for a couple of years. Not doin' me any good."

Joe took a close look at the saddle, and he had to wipe off a layer of dust. The leather was old and scratched up. Dried and cracked in places. But under the circumstances, it would do.

Next stop was the general store. He had intended to buy supplies to get through a winter in the mountains, but now his plans had changed. He needed clothes. Kate couldn't very well ride a horse far in that dress she was wearing. He bought some canvas range pants that he guessed to be her size, and a range shirt. She would need boots. Many cowhands were starting to buy theirs by mail order. Tracing their feet on a piece of paper so the boot maker could design one to fit perfectly. But at the general store there were six pair of riding boots in various sizes, and he found one pair that he thought might fit Kate.

He bought blankets and a length of oil cloth, as she would need a soogan. He bought cans of beans and peaches. He remembered once she said she preferred tea to coffee, so he bought a can of it. He grabbed some coffee for himself and two sacks of flour.

He also bought a box of ten gauge double-ought, and a box of cartridges for the rifle.

The clerk behind the counter noticed the smaller size of the clothes.

"You buying these for a boy?"

Sounded good enough, Joe thought. He said, "Yep."

"Looks like you're heading off on a long trip."

Joe nodded. "That we are."

Back at the livery, Joe rolled the clothes for Kate into the blanket, and rolled up the blankets and wrapped the oil skin around them. The saddle included a tattered pair of saddle bags, so he filled them and his own with the food supplies. It wouldn't be enough to get through the winter, but it would last a while.

Then he saddled both horses.

It was growing dark, which meant he still had a while to wait. He mounted up and rode to the Train Whistle. He had a hankering for one more taste of beer before he left town. It might be a long time before he tasted it again.

The bartender was the same from earlier in the day.

Joe said, "I'll take one of them Saint Louie bottles of beer."

The bartender pulled the cork and set the bottle in front of Joe.

"So," the man said, "change your mind about staying for the hanging?"

"Nope. Never did cotton to that sort of thing."

The saloon was busier than Joe would have expected for a week night. Probably folks in town for the hanging. A game of faro was going on at the back wall. The saloon girl from earlier was at a table with a young cowhand. He was talking and she was laughing, and looking at him like she had eyes only for him. The boy was young enough to think it was real.

Joe thought about Kate, and what he was about to do. The law wouldn't look on it kindly.

His plan was drastic, and not his first choice. He would have preferred to send a wire to Jack and get him down here. That boy was as clever with the law as Joe had ever seen, and he had the gift of flowery talk like Matt did. Jack could talk a dog into believing he was a cat. Joe had full confidence Jack would find a way to postpone the execution, and then get Kate's name cleared. But it would take at least two days to get Jack down here by train, and Kate didn't have that long.

Joe hadn't asked Kate if she had really killed Elias, because he knew her well enough to know the answer. But he realized, as he stood at the bar and sipped his beer, that it didn't really matter to him if she was guilty. He had looked into her eyes years ago and seen her soul, and it was the same way when he had visited her at the jail. If she killed her husband, there had to have been a good reason for it.

When the bottle was empty, he went to the hitching rail out front and the two horses.

"Get your rest, boys," he said to them. "We got us a long ride ahead."

He cut through an alley and used the outhouse, then stepped back into the saloon and ordered another bottle of beer.

He realized he wasn't afraid. What he was going to do tonight meant men might die. Bullets might fly. But he felt no fear. It was like Johnny had talked about, feeling a sort of calmness come over him before a battle.

Joe would like to have had Johnny with him tonight, and Matt. He could imagine Matt trying to talk him out of what he had planned, but then going along with it.

Joe thought about the long cross-country ride he had made with them, years ago. He wondered if he would ever see them again.

Kincaid had locked the door to his office at nine o'clock. There shouldn't be much need for a marshal on a Wednesday night. He stepped out at ten to walk his rounds, and told Abbott to keep the door locked until he got back.

Walking through the business section and checking all the doors to make sure they were locked took Kincaid a little more than an hour.

Two horses were tethered in front of the saloon,

both packed for traveling. Kincaid glanced in through the doorway and saw Joe McCabe at the bar, and figured the horses belonged to him.

Kincaid had seen the way Kate Compton had looked at Joe. There was love in her eyes. Not schoolgirl infatuation, or physical desire only. She was looking at him the way every man wants a woman to look at him at least once in his lifetime. Especially a woman as attractive as Kate.

Kincaid didn't know how a woman like Kate, who lived a life of wealth and finery, could have ever crossed paths with a wild and rough-looking man like Joe McCabe. But Kincaid knew if a woman ever looked at him the way she was looking at McCabe, Kincaid would not let her hang.

That was when Kincaid figured out what was going on. Both horses saddled. Joe at the bar, like he was waiting.

Kincaid was about to step into the saloon and talk to Joe. Maybe say, "Whatever you got planned, just don't hurt anyone. But whatever you're gonna do, you have to do tonight."

But then he thought better of it, and kept walking.

The night wore on. Joe chewed on a strip of jerky, and he ordered one more beer. It would be his last. He wanted to be clear-headed for what he was going to do tonight.

He had no watch, as he normally judged the time by the position of the sun or moon. But there was a small clock on the shelf behind the bar.

By 11:30, the saloon was emptying. The cowhand and his girlfriend-for-hire had left. The faro game had broken up.

Time for Joe to go, too.

He dropped three nickels on the bar to cover the price of the beer, and he stepped out into the night.

14

Once Kincaid was back at the office, he saw the kettle standing on the stove. He wanted another cup of coffee, because he would be getting no sleep tonight. He never did, the night before a hanging.

It had been a horrific murder. But Kincaid had looked into Kate's eyes and he didn't think she had done it. He had seen killers in his years as a lawman. He thought he knew a killer when he saw one.

Kincaid decided he was going to step outside for a moment. The outhouse was behind the building.

"Abbot, I'm going out back for a minute or two."

Abbot was at his desk with a newspaper spread over it. He nodded.

Kincaid said, "Keep that front door locked."

Abbott didn't look up from his paper. "I'll do that."

Kincaid stepped out into the night, letting the back door hang ajar.

He was in no hurry. Once he was done with the outhouse, he lit up a cigar and then walked to the back door, allowing himself to enjoy the night air.

He stepped in. Joe McCabe was standing in the center of the room, his scattergun held at his hip and aimed toward the doorway and the marshal. Kate Compton was beside Joe, and Abbott was at his desk, his hands cuffed behind him. His revolver was on his desk.

Joe said, "Howdy, Marshal."

"Well, I can't say I'm surprised," Kincaid said, taking the cigar from his mouth.

"You gonna give me any trouble?"

Kincaid shook his head. "Not at the moment. I'm going to have to hunt you down, though."

"I figured."

Kincaid took a draw from his cigar. "I'm gonna have to get together a posse. Probably take most of the morning."

He glanced at the clock on the wall. "I figure if you leave now you'll have a ten-hour head start. Make the most of it. Don't let me catch you."

Joe said, "What caliber gun you carry?"

"Forty-five. Why?"

Joe looked at Abbot. "How about that gun on the desk?"

Abbott said, "Forty-four forty."

"That's what I'm looking for."

Joe snatched the gun from the desk and tucked into the front of his belt.

Abbott said, "You can't take my gun."

"Just did."

Kincaid took another draw from his cigar. "Forty-four-forty must be the same caliber as that Winchester you had earlier. Takes the same cartridge."

Joe nodded. "Do I have to ask you to drop your gun?"

"Remember what you said about never turning over your weapons?"

Joe nodded.

"I've never turned my gun over, either."

Joe nodded again. "Fair enough."

Kincaid stepped aside, and Joe and Kate headed for the back door.

Kincaid said, "A ten-hour head start is the best I can give you."

"You won't find us. Ain't a man alive can find me if I don't want to be found."

"Keep her safe."

Kate said, "Thank you, Marshal."

Kincaid watched from the back door as Joe and Kate slipped around the back of the building and into an alley.

He had left McCabe the window of opportunity, hoping McCabe would take the hint. Kincaid figured McCabe would get the jump on Abbott without having to fire a shot. If Abbott had been a more competent deputy or a better fighting man, then Kincaid would have had to figure out a different plan, because he didn't want anyone killed.

Abbot was furious. He let out a string of profanity. "I can't believe you just let them go!"

Kincaid shrugged. "What would you have me do? Get myself shot?"

Kincaid reached into Abbott's vest pocket and fished out the key to the handcuffs. Abbott always kept his key in that pocket.

Kincaid said, "Do you really think I could have stopped that man? Do you really I think you and I together could have? All that would have happened is that we would have made him have to kill us. Didn't see any point in that."

Kincaid unlocked the handcuffs, and Abbott rubbed his wrists. The handcuffs had been a little tight.

Kincaid sat at the edge of his desk and took one more draw on his cigar. There wasn't much left of it.

He said, "Besides, do you really think she killed her husband? Do you think she has what it takes to cut a man's throat with a kitchen knife?"

Abbott said, "That ain't for us to decide. She was given a trial. A jury found her guilty."

Kincaid found himself looking at the kettle on the stove again. Maybe a cup of coffee would be good, even though there was no longer going to be a hanging the next day.

He said, "The intent of the law is good, but the law is written by men, and men are flawed. Each of us. As such, the letter of the law is often limited. Sometimes you have to look at the intent of the law if you want real justice. An innocent woman getting the noose is not what I call justice."

"Are you saying we have to use our own judgment instead of obeying the law?"

Kincaid grinned and shook his head. "Sometimes we

have to use that judgment. It gets easier to do when there's a scattergun pointed at you."

Abbott got to his feet and started pacing. "The job of a lawman is not to play judge and jury."

"No. But you still have to live with yourself."

"What makes you so danged sure she didn't do it?"

Kincaid looked at him. "Because I've been doing this job a long time. I've looked into the eyes of killers before. When I looked into her eyes, I wasn't looking into the eyes of a killer."

"Simple as that?"

Kincaid shrugged. "Sometimes that's all you have to go on."

He loaded some wood into the stove and struck a match. "Come tomorrow morning, I'll announce that Joe McCabe broke in here while I was out back, and got the jump on you, then got the jump on me when I came back in. I'll make the announcement around six o'clock, as though it just happened. Then I'll get that posse together and we'll go after them. We'll make every effort to find them, but I don't think we'll be able to."

"What's to stop me from going and getting my cousin right now?"

"Nothing. Do what you have to. That's what I did. But keep in mind, in the long run, you have to live with your decisions. The right decisions are often not the easy ones."

Abbott stood a moment, giving it all some thought

while Kincaid lit a fire in the stove.

Abbott didn't leave to go and fetch his cousin. He returned to his desk.

He said, "Who do you think really killed her husband?"

"We'll probably never know."

15

Joe led Kate along a worn trail for a few miles before they turned off and began traveling overland. The main trail was hard-packed enough from frequent use that the tracks of two individual horses wouldn't stand out.

Once they left the main trail behind, they cut through land that was as rocky as Joe could find. At one point, they found a stream that was running strong, and they rode through it for half a mile.

Riding along a streambed was tricky at night. Too many loose stones for a horse to slip on. The going was slow, but the water would wash away any tracks.

After a while they left the stream, and they kept the horses to a trot as they rode by moonlight. The sky was clear and the moon was three quarters full.

Joe kept the horses to a light trot. A good horse can go for hours at a pace like this, but every couple of hours he would stop and let the horses rest a bit.

Kincaid had said he would give Joe and Kate a ten-hour head start, and Joe was taking him at his word. He hoped to have covered fifty miles or more by then.

Kate was no horsewoman, but she remained in the saddle out of pure gumption. Her dress billowed out behind her, and her bottom bounced in the saddle so much she thought she might be bruised for a week. Her hair flowed behind her and she held onto the reins, though she really didn't know what to do with them. The horse she was riding seemed to know it was supposed to fall into place behind Joe's.

They rode most of the night. When Joe stopped the horses for a rest and helped her down out of the saddle, she collapsed on the ground.

"I didn't think it was possible to be so tired," she said. "I think I could sleep for a week. I didn't get a lot of sleep in the jail. The bed was hard as a rock, and it's hard to sleep when you can hear them building a gallows for you outside."

Joe squatted down beside her and glanced toward the east. The morning sky was coming alive with fiery streaks that were painted along a few strands of clouds. "We been riding about seven hours. You might as well get a little rest right now. We gotta ride most of the day, and then we'll make camp tonight and you can get some sleep."

She gave him a smile. Tired, but full of radiance. "I don't know how I could ever thank you. You came in out of nowhere, and literally pulled me from the jaws of death."

He shook his head. "That's what you do when you love someone. No need to thank me."

She reached a hand to his face, where the grizzly had caught his face.

"Those scars," she said. I'm sure you gave the bear what-for."

He nodded. "You might say that. He got a piece of me, but his fur keeps me warm in the winter."

He rose to his feet and began to loosen the saddles.

He said, "We'll let the horses breathe for a bit and graze a little if they want to. I call this here thing I'm loosening a cinch. My brother Johnny learned his horsemanship in Texas, and down there they call it a girth."

Kate didn't know quite what he was talking about but she didn't care. At the moment, her head was swimming from exhaustion and she was feeling overwhelmed at having Joe simply reappear in her life and rescue her from the gallows.

She said, "When I first met you, you were rescuing me from Indians. And now you're rescuing me again."

He grinned at her. "Seems like what I do, don't it?"

"And I am so very grateful."

Joe said, "I've got some clothes for you that might be better for riding than that there dress." He untied her soogan from the saddle and unrolled it, and he handed her the pair of men's pants and shirt, and the boots.

"I bought these for you in town. I hope they fit. I was kinda guessin' at the size."

"Oh, Joe," she said. "I hate for you to have gone to all of this trouble just for me. I'm truly not worth it."

He took her hand. "When you look at me, it's in a way no other woman has ever looked at me. I've seen it before. My brother Johnny has had two women look at him that way. My brother Matt has a woman in his life who looks at him that way. My nephews have married good women, and those gals look at them boys like that. I would do anything for you."

She was blinking back tears. "I have loved you, Joe, from the moment our eyes first met. I couldn't be with you, because I had promised myself to another."

"I fully understand."

"But I have found the human heart doesn't always go along with prior commitments. I belonged to Elias as far as commitment goes, but my heart always belonged to you."

He squatted down beside her again, and she rested her head on his shoulder.

"It's so beautiful out here," she said, looking off toward the east. "Do you think they're back there? The posse? On our backtrail?"

He shrugged. "Maybe. I did what I could hiding our tracks, but it was dark and I was in a hurry. If Kincaid is as good as I think he is, he'll find our trail. If he wants to."

"Do you think we can outrun them?"

"We're gonna have a huge head start on them. And I know the wild country. I have no intention of letting them have you."

Joe grabbed his rifle and did some scouting about on foot, mainly to give her the chance to get changed. When he returned, she was in the new clothes.

She said, "I've never dressed like a cowhand,

before."

He smiled. "I have to say, you look better'n any cowhand I've ever seen."

She stepped up to him. She said, "There's so much I want to say to you. And one thing I need to do. Something we never had the opportunity to do years ago."

"Now ain't the time.

"Yes it is. If those men catch us, I want to at least know that I kissed you when I had the chance."

Their lips touched. Gently at first, then a little more firmly.

"Just like I always dreamed of," he said.

She was smiling. "Your beard tickles."

"I can shave it off."

"No. I'll get used to it. I love you just the way you are."

Joe tightened the cinches.

She was going to discard the dress, but Joe said, "I don't want to leave any sign of us passing. A seasoned tracker might be able to find our trail, but I don't want to make it easy for them."

He rolled up her dress and the petticoats that went with it and tied them to the back of her saddle.

He said, "We got some hard riding ahead of us. You up to it?"

She nodded. "We Waddells are from hardy stock."

"I can see that. I saw it then, too, years ago."

"Where are we going?"

"A camp of mine, in the Big Horn Mountains."

16

Joe helped Kate up and into the saddle, then he mounted up and they continued on. A half hour later, the sun came fully into view.

Joe looked back at her. "You doing all right?"

She was bent over the saddle horn, like she was in pain. But she nodded. "I'm doing fine."

"No you ain't. You're about to fall over."

"I'm fine, really. I'd rather be in a little discomfort now, than be in a lot of discomfort later at the end of a rope."

He had to admit, she made sense.

They continued along. Behind them were miles of low, hills. Ahead of them were some ridges. They looked a dark purple in the morning light.

"We've been climbing up hill," she said.

Joe nodded.

She said, "Are we heading into those ridges?"

He nodded again. "They're not as close as they look. But that's where we'll make camp tonight."

"How far do you think we've gone from town?"

"Eighteen miles. Maybe a little further. And we've been making it hard for them. They're gonna have to spend time trying to find our tracks, like back at that little stream.

"Do you think Marshal Kincaid will be true to his word?"

Joe nodded. "My nephew Jack told me about him. He said Kincaid is a stand-up sort of man. Jack's a good judge of character."

Kate looked off toward the east. The sky overhead was clear. The thin line of clouds that had been there in the early morning light had blown away, but there was a heavier cloud bank to the northwest. She said, "Are those clouds coming our way?"

He nodded. "It's gonna rain."

She gave a long sigh and looked defeated. "After all we've been through, we're going to have to deal with the rain, too?"

"Rain's a good thing. It'll wash away our tracks. I don't think the rain will be on us until later this afternoon. We should be in the ridges. We'll find a place to hunker down for the night."

The wind was coming at them from the northwest, and it was chilly and damp. They pushed on.

They kept the horses to a light trot, but after a couple of hours Joe reined up.

"Best rest the horses for a bit," he said.

Not that he thought they needed it. But he thought Kate needed it.

The cloud cover now stretched across the sky, and the clouds were dark and gray.

"I figure it's about noon," he said. "That means you outlived your death sentence."

She couldn't help but smile. "I just hope you haven't

brought a world of trouble onto yourself for helping me."

He shrugged. "Been in trouble before. Reckon I will be again."

"But anything this severe?"

He nodded. He was thinking of Coleman Grant.

He said, "Once we know we've shaken that posse, and we've gotten you the rest you need, I'll tell you all about it."

After Kate had rested for a short while, they rode on. At one point, Joe opened a can of beans and they ate them cold.

By late afternoon, they were climbing the ridge. Pines stood tall about them one moment, then they would ride into an open area that was mostly rock and scattered patches of sage. They rode along the edge of a gravelly ravine, and then were back in a forest of pine again.

Joe found a section where the land behind them rose in a sharp, grassy bank. Pines stood straight all about them.

"This'll have to do," he said. "The trees will help shield us from the rain. We got a couple hours of daylight left, and I'll build us a lean-to."

Joe stripped the saddles off the horses and picketed them where they could graze for a while.

He took an axe from his bedroll, and began to hack at some pine poles. Thunder rolled in the distance.

"It's going to be a hard night," she said.

He shook his head. "Not at all. Trust me."

"Oh, I do, Joe. You're probably the one I trust most

in the world."

He cut pine poles and built a lean-to similar to the one he had built in the Big Horns. He worked quickly, because the wind was strong and cold, and he could feel the coming rain on the wind.

Kate stood, her arms folded in front of her to keep herself warm.

She said, "I wish I could help."

"Can you start a fire?"

"That's one thing I can do."

She gathered small sticks for tinder, and then collected some dry pine branches that had fallen. She braced each against the ground and then pushed down with a foot to break them to the proper length.

Joe had matches in his saddle bags, and by the time she had a fire going, his lean-to was built.

He said, "The fire won't last long in the wind and rain, but we should be able to get some hot coffee and heat up some beans."

He pulled the can of tea from his saddle bags. "And this is for you."

She looked at the tea and then at him.

She wanted to say so much. He could see it in her eyes. He touched the side of her face, then swept back a long strand of hair that was trailing across one cheekbone.

He said, "We'll have plenty of time."

She ate warmed beans like she had never eaten before, and she ate them directly out of the skillet. Joe had carved a spoon from a piece of pine wood during his stay in the Big Horns, and she used it.

She looked at him a little embarrassed. "I am afraid I'm eating like a pig. I even slurped a couple of times."

He was grinning. "Think nothing of it. We ain't in no high society dining room. We're here in the mountains. The rules of the world seem to fall away out here. Them rules, they just don't seem real to me. What's real is this." He waved a hand, indicating the clouds above and the trees about them.

When she was finished, Joe took the spoon and finished off what she hadn't eaten. He poured her a cup of tea and had some coffee for himself.

Then the rain came down. It was cold, and it pounded the earth. The fire went out in a smoking sizzle, and Kate and Joe ran for the lean-to.

Joe had positioned the opening of the lean-to so it faced away from the wind.

Kate looked up at the pine bough roof Joe had put together.

She said, "Will this thatching hold?"

"It'll be all right. The pines overhead will catch a lot of the water, and this roof should hold most of what slips through."

He had spread one set of blankets on the ground, and another for them to crawl under.

From the front of his belt, he pulled the revolver he had taken from the deputy in Cheyenne, and set it on the ground within reach. She said, "Is that the gun you took from the deputy?"

"Yep. It takes the same caliber as my rifle. Same cartridges. You know how to shoot?"

She shook her head. "I'm afraid I'm of little use out here in the wilderness."

He set his long knife and his scattergun beside the pistol, and then rested back on a folded blanket he and Kate were using as a pillow. She stretched out beside him.

"I'm so tired and sore from riding," she said, "Here we are, lying down on the hard ground, and yet it feels better than any bed."

She was quiet a moment, then said, "My life got turned around two months ago, when Eli was killed. I was the first to find him. And then I was arrested for the murder. It's like my life got snatched away from me, and it's been one topsy-turvy carousel since. And now, being here with you, it's almost like I have somehow come full circle."

"Yeah. I can see that."

"Joe, I have nowhere to go."

"Don't you have a home in Oregon? From what I understand, your husband and his brother made good money. When all the dust settles, I 'spect you'll go back to that life."

"How can I? My name will likely be on wanted fliers from Portland to San Francisco. And I'm not sure I really want to go back. That life never really felt like mine.

It felt like I was living out someone else's life. All I ever really wanted was a long-haired mountain man with the kindest heart I have ever known."

Joe wanted to kiss her again. But he tried to remind himself that she had been the wife of another man for a lot of years, and she had lost him just two months earlier.

He might not cotton much to the rules of society, but there was some territory it just wasn't right to tread. Despite the kiss earlier.

He said, "Don't you have children? I'm sure they'll miss you."

"No. Elias and I had none."

She went on to describe a life where she went through the motions of being a wife, but her heart was never really invested in the marriage.

She said, "Elias was a good man. I felt so bad for him, because he deserved a wife who could love him the way he needed to be loved. The way we all do. But I was not the one for him. Not really. And he wasn't the one for me. I realized that when I met you."

She drew a breath. "Elias and I rarely talked, those last few years. I think he knew there was someone else. He left me to myself, and I did the same with him. He would go off on business trips with his brother. They bought interests in a mine in Mexico, and were there four months one time. I had the house to myself. I would sit on the porch by day and look off at the sea, and I would sit by the fire at night and wonder about a certain mountain man."

"There weren't a day went by that I didn't think of you."

"And now I'm accused of Elias's death. Though we weren't in love, he was a good man. I can't imagine who could have done it. Who would have wanted him dead. And now I have no place to go."

Joe was quiet a moment, letting ideas trickle through his mind. Making sure what he was about to say was said right.

He said, "You're welcome to stay with me. I ain't got much. The past year I've been livin' mostly on the side of a mountain in the Big Horns. But you're welcome to share that life with me, if you're willin'."

"Joe, I think that's the kindest offer anyone has ever given me. I'm realizing that maybe I made a wrong decision years ago. The good Lord has essentially brought me back to the place where I made that decision, and now I have a chance to do it right. If you'll have me..."

"There ain't no question about that."

"Then I'm yours. Now and for always."

There was another kiss, then. He let his fingers lightly caress the side of her face.

"I'm afraid I must smell dreadful," she said. "I haven't been allowed a bath in three weeks, in that jail."

"I cain't smell much. Took a punch years ago. Broke my nose."

She laughed. At first just a chuckle, then an outright laugh. And he did, too.

Then she snuggled in next to him.

He said, "You warm enough?"

"Oh, yes."

They were quiet a moment. He was going to tell her that he thought the rain would let up by morning, and with their tracks washed away, they would ride in a direct route northeast toward the Big Horns. But he realized she was already asleep.

So he listened to her gentle breathing, and the rain hitting the ground outside. And he thought about how much his life had changed in just a day and a half.

17

Kate gradually rose to consciousness. She realized was alone in the blankets. She called out, "Joe?"

He stepped into the opening of the lean-to. He had a cup of coffee in hand. She was trying to blink her eyes into clarity. There was a gray light about them, and the air felt cold and damp.

"Is it morning?" she said.

He grinned. "It's afternoon. You done slept through most of the day."

"I slept through the day?"

He nodded. "That you did. I figured you needed the sleep, so I didn't wake you up."

She kicked off the blankets, and he reached down with a hand to help her up. She found Joe had a fire going.

She said, "What about the posse?"

"I don't think they're gonna find us. We have too many miles between us and the town of Cheyenne. A sight more than fifty. We're in the southern tip of the Absaroka Mountains. They ain't gonna follow us. The rain washed away our trail but good."

"What about the smoke from the fire? Won't they see it from a distance?"

Joe was burning pine and the fire was a little smoky. He glanced at the smoke and said, "Follow it up toward the sky."

She did.

"Notice how it kind of spreads as it thins out?"

She nodded. The smoke did just what he said it was doing. It rose maybe twenty feet then dissipated into a widening cloud of smoke and then was gone.

He said, "On days like this, when it's cloudy and misty, the smoke don't rise straight up like it does on clear days. And on a day like this, even if the smoke did rise up, you wouldn't be able to see it from too far away."

"You mean, we're free? We got away?"

He nodded. "We're gonna have to stay in hiding. We're fugitives. It means we'll have to hide in the mountains. There won't be any towns we can go to."

She was smiling. "As long as I'm with you, I don't care."

She spread her arms out about her and spun around. "Out here, in these mountains, I think I feel truly free for the first time."

Joe had a skillet full of baked beans heating in the fire. He said, "Supper should be ready in a few minutes. Or for you, breakfast."

She grinned. "I am so starved. Those beans smell heavenly. "And," she reached a hand to her backside, "I hurt in places I have never hurt before."

He laughed. "It's all them hours we spent in the saddle."

"How do you do it? You and your brother Johnny, when I first met you, you had ridden all the way from

California. And that other man, Zack Johnson."

"There's a way to stay in the saddle without it bruisin' up your backside. I'll show you."

"There's so much I have to learn, if I'm to live out here without being a burden to you."

"You'll learn it. I'll teach you."

He went to the edge of the lean-to for a flat slab of wood.

He said, "I made this for you while you were sleepin'."

He had carved a section of pine into a flat surface that was slightly concave.

"It can serve as a plate," he said. "It's kind of crude, but it'll work."

She smiled. "You are so resourceful."

He pulled the skillet from the fire and dumped some beans onto the plate, and handed it to her. She used his hand-carved spoon and dug into the beans like she hadn't eaten in a week.

When she realized what she was doing, she said, "I'm sorry. I'm making a beast of myself, just like last night."

He was grinning. "Don't be. Out here, we just eat up. We don't worry about what other folks think."

He ate from the skillet. When the beans were gone, he dropped a couple more chunks of wood on the fire. Then he sat cross-legged on the ground in front of the fire. From the fire, he pulled a twig that had a little flame dancing on the end, and he lit his pipe.

She said, "I remember when you rescued me the first time. We had to sit on the ground around the fire."

He nodded. "Ain't no chairs. The Indians don't use any. Nowadays, when I sit in a chair, it hurts my back after a while."

She sat in front of him and leaned back into him. He wrapped his arms around her.

She said, "I think I can get used to this."

They sat in silence for a while. The sky had grown dark, but here and there, stars peeked through the cloud cover.

"I think it's clearing up," Joe said.

"Oh, Joe, there's so much I want to say. So much lost time to make up for. So many years, when we should have been together."

He shook his head. "Things are as they're meant to be. I suppose I learned that from the Cheyenne. Our lives took the paths they were meant to take. And now the two paths have come back together."

"They sound like a wise people."

He nodded his head. "In many ways, wiser than the white man."

"So much has happened in such a short time. I feel so badly for Elias."

His arms were still wrapped around her, and she reached up to place one hand on one of his.

She said, "His body was shipped back to Portland,

and that's where he was buried. I couldn't even attend the funeral. I was being held in Cheyenne on no bail."

"No bail?"

She shook her head. "The district attorney convinced the judge that I was too much of a flight risk."

She couldn't help but chuckle. "I suppose, in the end, he was right."

Joe was grinning. He said, "Do you have any idea who killed him?"

She shook her head. "None a'tall."

Then she told him of that night. They had been renting a house, and were in separate bedrooms. They had been for years. He had been awake reading when she went to bed. She woke up hours later and the lamp was still burning in his room, and she found him dead.

She shut her eyes and gave a little, silent shudder. "It was so horrible, Joe. I had never seen anything like it. Blood everywhere. I screamed and ran out to get the marshal."

"When did he arrest you?"

"Not for two days. I took a room at the hotel. When the marshal and his deputy knocked on my door and told me they had to arrest me for the murder of my husband, it didn't feel real. I suppose I was still in shock from the murder."

She drew a slow breath. "Why would anyone want to kill him? He was a kind man. Always good to me, even though we had a loveless marriage."

"Did he have any other women?"

She shrugged. "It was said that he saw a woman in Portland. I never asked him, or pursued any inquiries on my own. I couldn't blame him."

Joe was silent a moment, letting a question roll over in his mind. A question he wanted to ask, but didn't know how to.

She didn't make him ask it. She said, "I never saw anyone outside of our marriage. I figure you were about to ask."

"I didn't know quite how to."

"Joe, you can ask me anything. Always."

He nodded his head.

She said, "I suppose, in a way, though, that I was always seeing someone else. Because you were always in my heart."

He had set his pipe on the ground. He reached one hand to it and took a draw. It had gone out. He set it back down.

He said, "When something bad is done to someone, and no one knows who done it, I find the easiest thing is to look at who benefits the most from it. Who would benefit the most from Elias's death?"

"Well..." She raised her shoulders in a long, sustained shrug. "No one would benefit from it. Not that I can see."

"With him dead, you would be his heir."

She nodded. "But he and I owned his half of the

business equally. I wouldn't be gaining anything. I don't know anything about business. His brother Jonah would have to run it all."

"So, who would your heir be?"

She thought a moment. "Elias and I have a will. We have no children, so everything would be left to Jonah."

She looked up at him. "Are you saying you think it was Jonah?"

"I don't know. What kind of man was he?"

She shrugged. "Not the most personable, I suppose. A good head for business, but Elias clearly had all of the charm. He was the one who made contacts and closed business deals. Jonah is his younger brother. He never married. But I remember him when he was a child. The Comptons and my family had adjoining farms. Elias and I grew up together. I can't imagine he had what it would take to slit his brother's throat."

"He could have hired it done."

She shuddered again. "I would hope not."

"Could it have been a robbery? Was anything missing?"

She shook her head. "To think, I was in the very next room."

"No sign of a struggle. That might mean he knew the attacker."

"No. Nothing missing. No sign of a struggle a'tall."

Kate was a little shaken. "To think Jonah could be capable of even hiring someone to do something as ghastly as that. And yet, with me out of the way, the entire family business falls to him."

"I'd like to see my nephews Jack and Tom go to work on this. Jack's a lawyer in Jubilee. Johnny's son. Tom is the town marshal. He's the son of my brother Matt. You ain't met Matt, yet. Jack and Tom are good at stuff like that."

"Do you think we'll ever know who did it?" she said.

"Don't see how. For us to go back wouldn't do no good. They'll just hang you, and I'll be locked up in Laramie for the rest of my life."

"What's in Laramie?"

"Territorial prison. And Tom don't have jurisdiction outside of Jubilee, and I remember Jack mentioned something about having to have a license to practice law in different places. He may not be able to work in Wyoming."

"The district attorney in Cheyenne didn't believe me at all. A man named Abbott."

Joe chuckled. "Yeah. His cousin was the deputy. Almost wet his pants when he looked up from his newspaper and saw me standin' there with my ten gauge aimed at his face."

She said, "I have to admit something. I have loved you for all of these years, but we have never been together as man and woman. And yet, with Elias dead barely two months, it somehow doesn't seem right. Like there should be a time of mourning. Then there's the fact that I haven't had a bath in three weeks. I haven't been this dirty since the wagon train, years ago. I can't have you touch me like this."

"When we get to the Big Horns, there's a place you can have a bath. A small pond fed by a natural spring. The water's cold, but it gets you tolerable clean."

"I have so much to learn about life out here. Campfires and mountain springs. How to ride a horse without injuring myself. I haven't shot a gun in my life."

"There's plenty of time to learn."

She became aware of a pair of glowing eyes just beyond the circle of firelight. She let out a gasp. "Joe! What's that?"

"Don't worry," he said. "He's a friend."

Joe held out his hand and a large gray wolf walked into the camp. It walked right up to Joe, and Joe began scratching its head.

"I was wonderin' where you were," Joe said to the wolf.

Kate was staring wide-eyed at the animal.

Joe said, "This is Poe. The name's a take-off on a Cheyenne word. Poe, this is Kate."

"That's a wolf!" she said. She was trying not to shout. "That's a full-grown wolf."

Poe was looking at her curiously.

"Yep," Joe said, "that he is. Reach over and scratch his head. He likes it right behind the ears."

She hesitated.

"Go ahead."

She said, "He won't eat me?"

Joe laughed. "No. He's a friend."

She reached over to him. The wolf gave her hand a sniff, then leaned in so she could start scratching him.

She said, "Oh, I have so much to learn."

18

Kincaid fired up the stove, and set a kettle of coffee on to boil. The morning was a little chilly and the stove heated the room up nicely.

The door opened, and in charged Orson Abbott, District Attorney. He was about forty and a little portly. His hair was receding at the corners giving him a long, sharp-looking widow's peak.

Deputy Abbott was at his desk with a newspaper open. It was the recent edition of the St. Louis Times. Only three days old. It had arrived on the morning stage.

The deputy said, "Morning, Orson."

The district attorney ignored his cousin. He said, "Marshal Kincaid, what are you doing here when your prisoner is still on the loose? I heard you had disbanded your posse, but I just had to see it with my own eyes."

Kincaid said, "I don't really have to answer to you. Keep that in mind. I answer to the mayor. But since you're asking so kindly..."

Deputy Abbott caught the sarcasm in his boss's voice, and turned his face away to hide his grin.

Kincaid continued, "Yesterday, once I had put the posse together, we spent a good part of the afternoon cutting for sign outside of town. We found nothing."

"Now, Marshal, the man is no ghost. He has to leave tracks behind him, like any man."

"I've known men like him before. Old scouts and such. They're mighty clever at hiding their tracks. So then it occurred to me that he might have covered his tracks by hiding in plain sight. The roads in and out of town are so hard-packed that they don't show fresh tracks very well. So we followed each road for a few miles. Near sunset, we found a trail of two riders that cut away from one road about eight miles outside of town and headed north. But it was too dark for us to ride any further."

The coffee pot started boiling, so Kincaid grabbed a potholder and lifted the kettle from the stove. "It rained all night. I rode out this morning and found what I expected to find. The rain washed away any tracks that were there. All we know is that they headed north. Presuming the two riders were the ones we were after. I figure it's a safe bet."

"So that's it? You're calling off the search?"

Kincaid looked at him. "Where would you have me look? Do you know how big the country is out there? I've already sent wires to any towns north and west of here. If he shows up, they'll see him. A man as wild-looking as he is won't be hard to notice."

Orson put his fists on his hips. "Why do I have the feeling your heart isn't in this?"

"It's not that my heart isn't in it. It's that I've done this job long enough to know two things. One, you can't take this sort of thing personally or let it eat you up. And two, most law-enforcement requires patience. A lot of it."

Orson stood for a moment, looking at him. Kincaid

poured a cup of coffee and went back to his desk.

Orson said, "I have put a lot of time and expense into that conviction. I'm not about to let her just disappear."

"Gotta be patient, Counselor."

"I order you to take some men and go out there, and do what you call *cutting for sign*."

"How far do you think they got before the rain?"

"Riding in the dark? Not far. He had to have had a place to wait out the rain. I don't think he's as far away as you might think."

"So you want me to form another posse and go riding around out there, hoping to find tracks. You're talking about potentially hundreds of miles of terrain. That's going to take some time."

"Then I suggest you get moving."

"My job, Counselor, is to be the marshal of this town. I can't very well do that if I'm out there, traipsing around the countryside. And besides, you can't order me to do anything. Like I said, I work for the mayor."

"There was a U.S. Marshal in Denver, recently. Hannibal Crane. They say he's like that marshal down in the Nations, Bass Reeves. He never lets one get away."

"I've heard of both names."

"I'm going to send a wire to Denver. And then I'm going to take a walk to Mayor Carey's office. You may not be aware of this, but Joseph Carey and I are good friends."

"Maybe he doesn't know you like we do."

The deputy grinned again, this time not bothering to hide it.

Orson said, "Maybe Mayor Carey and I will discuss hiring another town marshal, one who is more enthusiastic about doing his job."

Kincaid got to his feet. "It's not that I don't do my job, Counselor. It's that I don't like being told how to do it by men not in the chain of command. Now unless you have some official business to discuss, why don't you remove yourself from my office?"

Orson Abbott gave a long glare at the marshal. Kincaid figured Abbott liked to consider himself a man of power, and it irked him that he had no power in this office.

Abbott turned and stormed out, slamming the door behind him.

The deputy said, "He's gonna get you fired."

"He can try."

"You don't know my cousin like I do. He's sneaky, but he's determined. He almost always gets his way."

"Let him." Kincaid sat back down and reached for his coffee. "I can always do something else. I've been in this office for a long time. Maybe it's time for another man to have the job."

"That man he mentioned. The U.S. Marshal."

"Hannibal Crane."

"I've heard of him. What Orson said is true. He's never let a man get away. They say there's no one tougher."

Kincaid nodded. "I've heard that, too."

"Between him and Joe McCabe, which one would you put your money on?"

"You've met McCabe. You've seen the look in his eye. I would put money on him over any other man I've ever met."

19

Joe and Kate were surrounded by grassy hills that stretched off into the distance. Just to the north was an outcropping of rock, and a small stand of alders. To the northeast were some ridges, looking hazy in the distance. The beginning of the Big Horns.

When they stopped to rest the horses, Joe told Kate he was confident no one was on their back trail.

"But how can you be sure?"

He took off his hat. It was covered with a layer of fine, whitish dust. He shook it off and said, "See that dust?"

She nodded.

He said, "When you ride along when it's hot and dry like it is today, the horses kick up dust. That's why we're covered in it. You can see a cloud of it from a distance. It's even more so in places like Arizona and New Mexico. If you look behind us, you'll notice there ain't no clouds of dust at all."

She turned her gaze to their back trail. The land stretched away in grassy hills. Sage and junipers were scattered about.

She said, "I don't see any dust clouds at all."

He shook his head. "There ain't no one back there."

They walked a bit, to stretch their legs while the horses grazed.

She said, "You've spent time as far south as Arizona and New Mexico? I can't imagine you being that far from your mountains."

He nodded. "I roam far and wide sometimes. Worked as a deputy marshal for a while, down in Texas. The marshal's name is Austin Tremain. You might have heard of him."

She shook her head. "Can't say that I have."

"They're starting to talk about him the same way they do Bass Reeves, Bodie Hickman, Heck Thomas, and Hannibal Crane. Men like that."

"I wonder what your Marshal Tremain would say about you breaking a convicted murderer out of jail."

"I think he'd understand."

They came to a small stream. Arid hills of gravel and sage rose in the distance, but oaks and maples stood on both shores of the stream. Grass grew green and tall. Kate cupped both hands and dipped them into the stream, and brought the water to her mouth.

"Oh, it's cold," she said.

Joe nodded. "Drink up. The water's fresh. It's a lot better than what's in our canteens."

Joe said, "There's a couple hours of sunlight left, but we're not gonna reach the mountains today, and this here is about the best spot to camp between here and there."

He found a spot where the trees were thick toward the south and west. It was there that he cut wood from a deadfall to build a campfire.

"Those trees will block the light of the fire," Joe said. "Just in case. Any riders lookin' for us will be to the south or maybe west. The fire will be visible from the north and east, but there shouldn't be anyone there."

She said, "I feel a little guilty, with you doing all the work. There's so much I need to learn if I'm not going to be a burden to you out here."

"You know how to build a campfire. You built a good one at our last camp."

She nodded. "That I do. I learned on the wagon train, years ago."

She had meant to ask him something at their last camp.

"Your matches are covered in wax," she said. "Why?"

"Somethin' I do. I melt candle wax over my matches. Makes 'em water proof."

"That's clever. I wonder if it would work on cartridges to keep gunpowder dry."

He shook his head. "Wax on the side of the cartridge would make it not set right in the chamber. Might jam up a Winchester."

Kate said, "It seems that survival in the wild is part common sense, and part ingenuity. Always thinking, always looking for better ways."

He nodded. "That's what it's all about."

He had spotted a small game trail and wanted to see if he couldn't rustle them up some supper. He took his rifle and said he would be back by nightfall.

Kate found the stream looked inviting, and she felt so dirty. She estimated the stream to be maybe fifteen feet wide, and it looked maybe two or three feet deep. The area seemed secluded and she was tempted to peel off her clothes and climb in. Maybe she would if Joe were still here, but she had to admit she felt a little scared. Out here, in the middle of nowhere. Alone.

Well, not quite alone. The wolf was standing nearby.

"Poe," she said. "I would really like a bath. But maybe not today."

She built a fire, and then she sat on the ground in front of it. She sat like Joe did, with her knees crooked and her ankles crossed.

"Look at me," she said to the wolf. "Sitting on the ground like a genuine Indian."

She gave a long sigh, and looked about at the trees. A light wind was kicking up and the branches were waving a bit. The sky overhead was blue with some thin, feathery clouds.

"It's so beautiful here," she said. "And yet I can't help but think about how strangely changed my life has become over just the past few months."

The wolf was looking at her. Kate couldn't help but laugh. She was talking as though the wolf could understand her. And yet, something in the eyes of the wolf made her think he almost could.

She heard a gunshot. It sounded like it was nearby.

She wished Joe was here.

Then she thought maybe it was Joe who had fired the gun. She had a fear that men from Cheyenne had caught up with them. But there were no more shots.

She went to her saddle bags and pulled out the revolver. Joe had stuffed it in there when they broke camp that morning.

She said to Poe, "I don't really know how to use this. But I feel safer with it in my hand."

Joe came back with a small deer over his shoulder. "We're gonna eat good tonight."

By dark, a leg of the deer was on a spit over the fire. Joe chewed on a chunk that he held speared on the end of his knife. Kate ate from the improvised plate he had made.

Poe had filled his belly with raw deer meat, and then he curled up on the ground by the fire.

Joe said, "That there stream is called Shell Creek. It comes out of the Big Horns. By tomorrow night, we'll be at my little camp in the mountains."

"In some ways, none of this feels real," she said.

Joe nodded. "Know what you mean. A lot has happened in a short time."

"Joe," she looked at him. "You rescued me without even questioning my innocence or guilt."

He nodded. "That's what happened."

"You never asked."

"Didn't need to."

"May I ask why? I mean, it had been so many years since you had seen me. How did you know—how could you know for sure that I am innocent?"

"I know you. People can sometimes change on the surface, but their heart is the same. I figured if you had killed him, it had to be for a good reason. Either way, I weren't gonna let you hang."

"Did you know you must be the sweetest man I have ever known?"

He chuckled. "You've said that kind of thing before. I don't see it, but I guess I'm glad you do."

When they were done eating, Joe tied the remainder of the deer carcass to a rope and suspended it ten feet off the ground from the branch of an oak tree.

"To keep the critters from it," he said.

They unrolled their soogans and spread them on the ground side-by-side.

She said, "I can't wait to get to your camp in the mountains. To begin our lives together."

"Me neither. One thing that's botherin' me, though. We ain't legally married, and I don't see how we can be. We're gonna have to avoid towns and settlements for a long time."

"What'll we do for supplies?"

"Prob'ly ride north, to Johnny's ranch, every so often. See if he can help get us what we need."

As they stretched out in their blankets and looked up at the stars, Joe told her about how after they had delivered her to Elias and the wagon train, he and Johnny and Zack Johnson rode north to the Crazy Mountains and found a small valley.

"We spent the winter there with a small band of Shoshones. Johnny ended up goin' back, and built a ranch there."

"We heard his name mentioned, from time to time. And the town of Jubilee. Jonah actually went to Jubilee last year, and he and Elias bought interest in a mine."

Joe nodded. "I heard that talked about in Cheyenne. Jubilee had one of the bigger gold strikes in Montana a few years ago."

A horse shifted a hoof. Joe looked over to the horses, in case they were getting nervous about something that might be out in the darkness. He saw they were still standing calmly, their heads lowered. The wolf was still dozing by the fire. Crickets were chirping. Joe decided there was nothing out there that shouldn't be. He rested his head back.

He said, "So, Elias and his brother went from farmers to big businessmen."

She nodded. "We were farmers back in England, and that's what we all did at first when we arrived in Oregon. We built cabins, and we began farming. Potatoes by summer and alfalfa by winter. Then Elias and Jonah had a chance to go into business, and they took it. We had an unusually profitable alfalfa crop our second year in Oregon, and they bought into a shipping firm. And the firm did well. Within a few years, they owned the entire business, and then they bought into a lumber operation. Then a cattle ranch.

"And yet through all of it, not a day went by that I didn't think of you. That I didn't hope you were finding the love of a good woman. The love you deserved."

"Never did. I've loved only two women in my life. One of them's you."

"Who's the other?"

"A young Cheyenne girl, years ago. Long before I met you."

"You've been alone for so long."

"Never all the way alone, though. I carried with me the memory of you."

She snuggled into him. "Maybe we won't be married by a preacher, but I consider myself married to you in my heart."

She then propped herself up on one elbow, and she gave him a wicked grin, the firelight flickering against her face. "And once I've had a chance to properly bathe in that pond you mentioned, so I don't smell like something that died days ago, I intend to be oh-so good a wife to you. After all, we have a lot of years to make up for."

"Gotta say, I like the sound of that."

20

They found Joe's dugout cabin the way he had left it. He lit a candle and took a look inside, in case any critters had taken up residence. None had. There were cob webs, though.

He said, "It's way too small for the both of us. I'll set about building us a proper cabin, so you'll have a kitchen, and we'll have a bunk to sleep in."

"What'll we sleep in while the cabin is being built?"

He looked to the lean-to. "Right there. That's all we'll need till cold weather sets in."

The thatching was brown and dry. He would have to cut fresh pine boughs in the morning.

That night, Joe built a big campfire. The nights here in the mountains were a little chilly, compared to down in the flatlands where he and Kate had been riding.

Kate was in her range shirt and pants. Earlier in the day, Joe had introduced her to the mountain spring where he did his washing. While she was in the water, he soaked her clothes and scrubbed them against some rocks. Now her clothes were dry and she was freshly bathed.

"I feel like a new woman," she said. "That water was so invigorating."

Joe had taken a swim in the water, too, and he had offered again to shave off his beard.

"No," she said, "I love you just the way you are."

Kate had found some wild onions and she stirred them into a skillet of beans while another haunch of the deer Joe had shot the day before was roasting on a spit. They were going to have two courses this night.

"Tomorrow," Joe said, "I'll show you how to shoot a rifle."

"It's such a big gun. Won't it knock me over?"

Joe shook his head. "It's all in the way you hold it. I'll show you. And I'll show you how to track a deer."

When they were finished eating, Kate stepped into the lean-to. Joe added some more wood to the fire. He checked on the horses that were in their lean-to. In the morning, he would take them to a meadow he knew of and let them graze.

Poe was puttering about, looking bored.

"Look, wolf," Joe said. "I appreciate your company, but tonight might be a good night for you to go roam the woods."

After a time, Kate stepped from the lean-to wrapped in a blanket. Joe could see her shoulders were bare, and he had the impression she was wearing the blanket only.

Poe seemed to get the hint, and he trotted off into the darkness.

Joe walked up to Kate. Her hair was loose and falling down her back in tight curls.

She looked into his eyes. No words needed to be said.

She turned and stepped back into the lean-to, and Joe followed her.

21

The following morning, Kate was in her range shirt and canvas pants. She held Joe's Winchester to her shoulder. He wrapped his arms around her from behind, helping her position the rifle.

They were in a meadow. The horses were grazing a hundred feet behind them. At the other side of the meadow was an old pine with a thick trunk, and it was serving as Kate's target.

Joe stepped back from her and said, "Pull the rifle tight against your shoulder. Now place your left foot a little forward and lean your weight into it."

She did as he said. "Why are you standing behind me? Afraid I'll shoot you?"

"Nope. You stand behind someone when they're shooting so the gunshot won't hurt your ears as much."

"That works?"

He shrugged. "Seems to."

"Okay, what now?"

"Squeeze the trigger. Don't jerk it, just give it a controlled squeeze."

She did. The rifle went off. The recoil knocked her backward, and Joe caught her. A cloud of gun smoke was in the air.

She was laughing, and Joe was too.

She said, "I don't think I'm cut out to be a

gunfighter."

"You gotta give it time. You're gonna do fine."

Joe shot a deer that afternoon, and he showed her how to gut and skin a carcass. He fixed up the little smokehouse he had made, and began smoking some of the meat for the winter.

As the days passed, Joe cut some logs and used the horses to pull them to the camp.

"We'll build our cabin right here," he said to Kate, looking at a flat area a hundred or so feet from the campfire. "I'll make a chimney out of rocks. We'll need big 'uns, and the horses can help me haul 'em up here. I'll also use the rocks I made the small chimney with in my dugout."

She worked at smoking meat. Joe showed her how to cure and tan deerskin, and after a while she was able to make herself a buckskin dress. The hem fell to her knees.

"You look like a gen-u-ine Cheyenne princess," Joe said.

She looked down at her bare calves and ankles. "These Cheyenne girls certainly showed a lot of leg, didn't they?"

He grinned. "I never heard a Cheyenne man complain about it."

"I'm sure not."

"You should see what the Cheyenne gals wear in the summer."

"Do I dare ask?"

"A grass skirt and not much else."

She gave him a look like she didn't quite believe him. He started laughing. Joe didn't laugh often, but when he did, it was a roaring belly laugh.

One night, they were in their blankets in the lean-to. He was on his back and her head was on his shoulder.

He didn't know if she was asleep, but he had a thought and wanted to share it.

"You know," he said, "I thought about this kind of thing a lot, over the years. What it would be like to go to sleep with you right here with me, and to wake up to you every morning."

She nodded her head. "Me too."

"Never thought it would happen. Now that it has, you'd think I'd be jumping in the air and screaming out yelps and *yahoos* that would echo through the mountains."

She chuckled.

He said, "But somehow, I feel calm. Like this is the way it's supposed to be."

"It feels natural."

"Yeah," he said. "That's just the way it feels. Natural."

The summer days passed. Some days, Joe worked on the cabin, and others he and Kate went hunting. She got so she could handle his rifle well. She also practiced with the revolver, holding it with both hands.

"You don't sight in with it, like you do a rifle," Joe

said. "You just point and shoot. I've seen Johnny sight in with one, but he's the only one. I've seen him make shots you'd have to see to believe."

"So the stories they say about him are true?"

He nodded. "Most of 'em."

"I saw him fight that Indian who had kidnapped me, years ago. It was ferocious."

One night, Kate was standing in her buckskin dress by the campfire. She held her hands out to warm them.

She said, "It gets so cold here in the mountains, in the summer."

Joe grinned. "Wait till you see winter."

"One day is so much like another. It's so idyllic. I can see why you love life in the mountains so much. I've long ago lost track of even what day it is."

He nodded. He was sitting by the fire with his long Indian pipe in one hand. "That's the way of it, out here."

"Do you even know what month it is?"

He nodded. "You learn to tell by things like the stars at night, and the path of the sun by day. It's closer to the southern horizon in the winter months, and travels higher into the sky by summer. I figure we're somewhere in the second or third week of July."

Kate slept easily and peacefully that night, as she had every night since Joe had brought her to the mountains.

Poe wasn't happy that night, though. He often slept in the lean-to with Joe and Kate, and sometimes out by the fire. But that night, he paced between the fire and the shelter.

Joe had been sleeping, and he woke to find the wolf pacing.

"What is it, boy?" Joe said.

The wolf looked off into the darkness.

Joe said, "Somethin' out there?"

Joe looked over to where the horses were picketed. They looked restful. If something was in the darkness that shouldn't be there, they would have been reacting to it.

Joe grabbed his scattergun, and he went to the fire and put on some more sticks. Poe went over to him and Joe scratched the wolf's head.

Joe looked at the rawhide strip around the animal's neck and said, "That there rawhide is getting to be in bad shape. I've gotta make you a new one."

The wolf looked off into the darkness again, in the same direction of earlier.

Something's out there, Joe thought. *Ain't bothering the horses, and the crickets were still chirping. But Poe ain't happy about something.*

The following morning, when the eastern sky was only beginning to lighten, he told Kate about it.

He said, "The horses weren't bothered, but I trust Poe's judgment."

"What are you going to do?"

"Go take a look. See what might be out there."

"Should I be scared?"

He shook his head. "Not till we know what it is. Might not be a threat a'tall."

He left her at the camp with the pistol. He pointed to Kate and said to the wolf, "Stay."

The wolf sat by Kate.

She said, "I think he understands."

"He seems to understand a whole lot."

She said to Joe, "Be safe."

He nodded. "I ain't going far. If you wanna get breakfast going, I'll be back in a little while."

He headed into the woods, and the wolf stayed at Kate's side.

Joe was on foot. Johnny, Matt and his nephews were all cowboys and preferred to go everywhere on the back of a horse. Bree was that way, too, and that tall jasper she married. But there were times when a man needed to move quietly and was better off afoot.

Joe was in his buckskin boots. His long knife was at his side, and his Winchester was in one hand.

He needed a look at the land down below. He knew of a rocky cliff a quarter mile up the ridge, and that was where he headed.

He didn't want to skyline himself, so he ducked low as he stepped out onto the cliff. Once he was near the edge, he dropped down to one knee.

It was daylight now, and from the cliff he had a view of the ridge below, and he could see the smoke of the fire rising up from his and Kate's camp.

He could see down the ridge, and the open, grassy expanse that began down below and stretched for maybe a quarter of a mile, and he had a good view of the next ridge beyond.

He could see smoke rising from the base of that ridge. He figured it must be a large campfire.

Someone was down there. A large campfire could mean a large group of men. Maybe cowboys from one of the ranches west of the Big Horns. But he had to go down there. He had to be sure.

22

Joe told Kate his plan. He intended to ride down the ridge and have a look at who was down there.

"I want to go with you," she said.

"I don't think that's wise."

She stood before him in her doeskin dress, and a pair of rawhide boots she had made.

He said, "It could be dangerous. We don't know who it is down there. It could be nothing. Cowboys doing some mustanging. But we should be careful. When you're on the run like we are, any mistake could be deadly."

"If it could be dangerous, then that's why you need me along. I'm not like I was when I first came to these mountains. You've been showing me how to track and how to shoot."

He nodded his head. They had been here a couple of months and she was learning fast.

She said, "You shouldn't have to go into a potentially dangerous situation alone."

He grinned. "I been doing that kind of thing alone for a lot of years."

"Well, you're not along any longer."

Joe let the fire burn down low so it would be less visible from a distance.

Joe saddled both horses. He had made Kate a pair of buckskin pants like his own. He figured it would easier for riding. She stepped out of the lean-to wearing the buckskins, and she was in the range shirt Joe had bought for her back in Cheyenne.

He couldn't help but smile. He said, "I didn't think it possible, but you look like a real desperado."

She gave him a smile back. "Well, that's what I am."

"Dang purtiest one I ever seen, though."

He handed the revolver to her. "This'll do you more good than me, if it comes to a shooting match. I'll be relying on my shotgun and my rifle, because of my hand. In fact, you should keep it with you all the time. We can consider it yours."

She checked the loads, like he had shown her how to do, and then she tucked it into the front of her buckskins.

"If we ever set foot in an actual town again," she said, "I'm going to have to get a holster."

Joe had to admit, she was becoming a good shot with a pistol. As good as he ever was before his hand got shot.

They mounted up.

Joe said, "We'll go down the mountain single file. I'll go first. Keep your eyes going from one side of us to the other, and take a glance behind us every minute or so. Don't watch specifically for a rider. Watch for anything that moves."

She nodded.

He said, "If we have to talk, don't whisper. A

whisper makes a rustling sound that can sometimes carry farther than talking low and quiet."

Joe had said much of this kind of thing before. By the fire at night, Kate would get him talking about the wilderness and how to survive here.

One night she even asked how it felt to kill a man.

He had said to her, "You don't need to know that kind of thing. You ain't no gunfighter."

"Well, maybe I'm becoming one. You used a word, one time, describing what you and your brothers are."

"Gunhawks."

"Well, maybe I'm becoming a lady gunhawk."

Joe grinned. "That's what my niece Bree calls herself."

"Now you have two in the family."

They rode down the side of the mountain, keeping their horses to a walk. Joe watched directly ahead of them and to either side, looking for any sign of motion around them, and he scanned ahead for tracks. He rode with his rifle across the saddle bows, and in its sheath on his back was his scattergun.

He glanced back at Kate. When they had first left Cheyenne, it was all she could do to remain in the saddle. Her butt bumped on the saddle with every step the horse took. Now she rode easily, like she was born to it.

The sun was three hours in the sky as they reined up at the edge of the trees, at the foot of the ridge. Joe pointed out to Kate the smoke rising behind the trees, near the foot of the ridge facing them.

"I'm gonna go from here on foot," he said. "But I don't want to leave the horses unattended. If we lose them horses, we'll be in real trouble. I need you to stay with 'em while I go take a look at the camp."

She said, "How long should I wait for you before I go look for you?"

"Don't come looking for me. If I don't come back, then it means those men are dangerous. Ride north, to the town of Jubilee. Find my brothers. They'll know what to do."

"I don't want to just leave you."

He shook his head. "If I don't come back, it'll be because I'm dead."

"I hate the sound of that."

He shrugged his shoulders. "This is the life I lead. There's good to it, but there's some that's not so good."

He handed her his rifle. "I won't be needing this."

He started away on foot.

"Joe," she said.

He looked back over his shoulder at her.

She said, "Be careful."

"Always am, Sweetie."

The grassy expanse between the two ridges was more than a quarter mile, she estimated. The grass still had a little springtime green, but much of it was now brown. It stood nearly to Joe's belt.

She watched as he ran. He kept low, and he stopped

every so often, dropping to one knee and looking around.

For a large man, he ran lightly and easily, and he covered the distance in less time than she would have figured.

When he stepped into the trees, he seemed to vanish. Now all she could do was wait.

At the edge of the forest, the trees were far apart and some grass grew. The horses were chewing on it. Kate considered loosening their cinches so they could breathe more easily, but then thought better of it. She wanted the horses ready should she and Joe need to ride away on short notice.

She pulled out the pistol and checked the loads again. Not that she needed to, but it gave her something to do. Then she tucked it back into the front of her buckskins and stood at the edge of the trees with Joe's Winchester in her hands.

She remained still. Joe had taught her motion can attract the human eye.

Then motion caught her own eye, down to her left. Poe had come out of the woods and walked toward her. The wolf looked at her like he fully understood what was going on.

They stood together and watched the woods beyond the grassy expanse, waiting for Joe to return.

23

The man stood by the campfire, a tin cup of coffee in one hand. He had thick sideburns that were a steel gray, and a matching mustache. He normally kept them neatly trimmed and the rest of his face cleanly shaved, but he had been on the trail for more than a week and his chin was covered with stubble.

He wore a hat with a wide, flat brim and a corduroy coat with a sheepskin lining. Even in the summer, nights and early mornings in the mountains could be chilly.

A revolver was holstered at his left side and turned for a crossdraw. Pinned to his shirt under his coat was a badge.

Beside him was a man with a long face and squinty eyes. He was holding his hands to the fire for warmth.

He said, "Marshall, how much longer we gonna be traipsin' about these mountains?"

"Quit your griping. You're being paid."

The man with the long face shook his head. "This is one of the hardest ways I've ever earned my money."

A man across the fire held a coffee cup in one hand. He had a mustache that was showing some gray. He was in a Boss of the Plains hat and leather chaps, and on his boots were spurs with big rowels.

He said, "I used to ride with drovers that brought herds up from Texas to the railroad. You want to see work, *that* was work. This here thing we're doing, riding through the mountains looking for a fugitive, is like a vacation compared to that."

"You sure he's out there?" the long-faced man said.

The marshal nodded his head. "Joe McCabe has been selling horses to the Lovell Ranch. Horses that were most likely caught in these mountains. It's good money he and that woman are here."

The face of a fourth man was bronzed from the sun and deeply lined. His cheekbones were high, and he had a hawk-like nose. His hair was black and fell to his shoulders.

The long-faced man looked at him and said, "How sure are you that McCabe's in these mountains?"

The man with the black hair shrugged but said nothing.

"Marshal Crane, why do we even have this Indian scout with us?"

The marshal said, "Because he's Cheyenne, and Joe McCabe spent time among the Cheyenne. We need a man with us who thinks like a Cheyenne."

The man in the chaps said, "I rode with a man named Goullie once, for the Carerra ranch down in Texas. He said he knew the McCabes years ago, when they all worked on a ranch together. He said the McCabes are not to be trifled with. He said they are three men you don't want to be on the wrong side of a fight with."

The marshal took one last sip of coffee and tossed

the dregs into the fire.

He said, "All right, men, let's put this fire out and saddle up."

He looked at the Cheyenne. "We riding east again today?"

The Cheyenne shrugged his shoulders. "Might as well. See what we can find."

"All right. East it is, then."

The Cheyenne turned his gaze beyond the camp. They were surrounded by tall pines, and about two hundred feet away was a stand of short, fat cedars. The wind was blowing toward the cedars, and the scent of the man standing there would not be caught by the horses. As the Cheyenne looked toward the cedars, he made eye contact with Joe McCabe.

The Cheyenne then turned away, saying nothing, and went to saddle his horse.

24

Joe stood motionless while the men mounted up. They turned their horses into the trees, heading to the open glade between the ridges.

Joe knew Kate and the horses were hidden at the other side of the glade. Kate was new to life in the wild, and Joe hoped she wouldn't panic when the men rode out of the trees. From what they had said, they would be turning their horses east.

Joe ran to the edge of the pines and waited. A little further down, the marshal rode out into the open glade, keeping his horse to a walk. Then came the man with the long face, then the former cowhand, and finally the Cheyenne.

The cowhand had mentioned the name Goullie, a name Joe hadn't heard in a long time. He hoped Goullie was doing well.

Joe waited while the men rode away. After about a quarter of a mile, the grassy area between the ridges rose up in a small incline. As the riders topped the hill and kept on riding, they became lost from sight. That was when Joe left the trees and ran across to Kate.

She was still here, with the horses. Poe was with them.

She said, "I saw the riders, but I hadn't heard any gunshots so I figured they hadn't seen you."

"One did. Looked right at me but didn't say a word. An Indian scout. They called him a Cheyenne."

"Do you think he really is Cheyenne?"

"Hard to tell. He looks Indian, but he's wearing white-man clothes."

"Who are those men?"

"A posse. They called the lead rider Marshall Crane. He can't be a town marshal. He wouldn't have any jurisdiction out here. Not that it hasn't stopped lawmen in the past."

"Maybe he's a U.S. Marshal."

"The thought crossed my mind. There's a Hannibal Crane who's a U.S Marshal. Have you heard the name?"

She shook her head.

He said, "They say he has never let a fugitive get away."

She looked scared, but there was no panic in her eyes. She said, "Let's make this the first time he fails."

"We have to get away from here. Let's go back to our camp and pack up. I want to put miles between us and these mountains before sunset."

They mounted up.

Kate said, "But if we leave these mountains, where can we go? To your brother's ranch?"

Joe nodded his head. "For starters. We can't stay there long, though. Wouldn't be fair to bring the law down on them. But I have an idea where we can go."

They rode up the ridge the same way they had

ridden down—in single file. They rode in silence. Poe would run ahead for a while and then return to them. Scouting ahead, Joe figured. A dog and a wolf were two critters who were a lot smarter than folks gave them credit for.

Once they were at their camp, they began rolling up their soogans.

"I'm going to miss this place," Kate said. "It's been like our own personal little paradise. It felt like we were the only people in the world. It's so sad that reality has to catch up with us."

"We'll find another place like this." Joe was tying his soogan to the back of his saddle.

"Do you have a place in mind?"

Joe nodded. He was about to tell her when Poe began growling. His back hairs were up and he was facing toward the woods.

Joe held a hand up, which Kate knew meant for her to be silent. He then reached up and slid his scattergun from the sheath on his back. She still had the revolver tucked into the front of her buckskins, so she pulled it free.

A rider was coming. Joe could hear the sound of sticks breaking as hooves stepped down on them. Pine trees were forever dropping dead twigs and small branches. A man afoot can step around them, but a rider didn't have that option.

The rider came into view. It was the Indian scout from the small posse. Joe held the scattergun at his left hip, gripping it with both hands, his left index finger on the trigger. Kate brought the pistol out to full arm's length, cocking the hammer back as she did so.

Joe said to the Indian, "That's far enough."

The man held up his hands. "I come alone. I told them I would do some scouting. I rode up here because I saw your fire last night. They didn't see. Like so many white men, they wouldn't see a bear until it was on top of them."

"You didn't tell them about me. Why?"

"Because I know the name Joe McCabe. I am Cheyenne, and I know you are, too."

The morning fire had been fully put out, but a coffee kettle was standing by the remains.

The man said, "Is there any coffee left?"

Joe nodded. "It's cold by now."

"Doesn't matter. I have been around white men too long. I've taken on some of their ways."

Joe chuckled. "Climb on down. Help yourself to what's left."

The man swung out of the saddle and dug a speckled enamelware cup from his saddle bags.

He said, "They call me Tom Spotted Owl, but in the old days, the Cheyenne called me just Spotted Owl."

He knelt by the fire and filled the cup.

Kate said to Joe, "He said you were Cheyenne. I know you told me you joined the tribe, but you're still a white man."

Spotted Owl took a sip of the cold coffee. "There are only two kinds of people. Tsitsistas and everyone else."

Joe grinned. "Ain't heard that word in a long time."

Kate said, "What's it mean?"

"Tsitsistas. It's what the Cheyenne call themselves."

Spotted Owl nodded his head. "White man have strange ways of looking at people by the color of their skin."

Joe said, "Most Indian tribes only care about which tribe you belong to. Even when they say *white man*, they don't care so much about color. What they care about is they don't belong to the tribe."

"How fascinating," Kate said.

"When I joined the Cheyenne, I became one of them."

Spotted Owl said, "I won't lead law men to one of the few Cheyenne who still runs free. I took the job as scout to get off the reservation. But I won't help them find you."

"Where are they now?"

"East of here, and north."

"If you keep them going in that direction, I would appreciate it."

"Where will you go?"

"North, and west."

"They won't find you. I'll make sure of it."

"I'll owe you."

Kate said, "Do you know why they're after us?"

Spotted Owl nodded. "They say you killed your husband."

"And yet still you help us."

"White man law not my law. If you kill your husband, you must have had a good reason."

"I didn't kill him. I don't know who did but I have my suspicions."

"If you didn't kill him, then there is even more reason for me to help."

Spotted Owl finished his coffee and mounted up.

Joe said, "We'll be out of these mountains by tonight."

"I'll keep the marshal going east. He won't find you."

"You will be welcome at my fire anytime."

Spotted Owl nodded and turned his horse away from the camp. Joe and Kate watched him ride away.

Kate said, "I'm beginning to think the Indians know more about honor than most white people ever will."

"Indians are like anyone else. Some are good and some ain't. Remember that one who kidnapped you, years ago. And some tribes know more about honor than others."

Joe went back to tying his soogan to the back of his saddle. He said, "We gotta ride. It's gonna be long and hard, the way it was when we first busted you out of jail. We'll be making cold camp every night until we get to the Crazies."

"The Crazies?"

"The mountains where Johnny has his ranch. A long valley. You'll see."

Kate swung into the saddle and so did Joe. He allowed himself one last look at the camp, and realized that even though he seldom allowed himself to give into sentiment, he would miss this place, too.

The lean-to was standing strong, with fresh green pine boughs that he had re-thatched it with just the day before. His dugout cabin was still there, against the side of the slope. Not far away was the partially-built cabin he and Kate were going to share.

He said, "I was foolish to bring you here. I should've known it would only be a matter of time before they found us. We need to go much further away."

"You said you have a plan in mind."

Joe nodded. "A few years ago, we broke a man out of a Mexican prison. Me, Zack Johnson, and my nephew Dusty. One of Johnny's sons. The fastest and best I ever seen with a gun. Even better'n Johnny. We took that man north, to the Canadian Territories. A place called Bow River Valley. We hid out there for a while."

She was looking at him with a smile of wonder. "You do lead the most interesting life."

He grinned. "I have my moments."

"So, is this Bow River Valley where we're headed?"

He nodded. "After we stop at Johnny's and get some supplies."

He let his gaze drift over their camp one more time,

then he turned his horse away. "Come on. We got a lot of miles to cover."

25

Hannibal Crane was out of his element in the Bighorn Mountains. He had been a lawman for much of his life and he knew how to follow a set of tracks. But he was not a man of the wilderness. The Big Horns were about as remote as you could get. Just a few years earlier, this had been Sioux Indian country. Custer had died not far from here.

But Crane was no fool. As out of his element as he was, he knew his Indian scout was leading him nowhere.

The scout returned near sunset. Crane and his men were setting up camp when Tom Spotted Owl rode in.

Dern, a long-faced man who had large, jagged teeth, reminding Crane of a possum when he smiled, said, "Where you been?"

"Scouting," the Indian said.

"Did you find any sign of McCabe?"

Tom shook his head. "Nothing."

Crane had the feeling the Indian knew a lot more than he was letting on. But then, most Indians gave him that feeling. Like they were somehow superior, even though the white man had won every war with them. Confined them all to reservations. Except for the Apache, but Crane was confident they would be defeated soon.

"Boys," Crane said, "this has gone on long enough. We're no closer to finding McCabe than we were days ago. For all we know, he's not even in these mountains. In the morning, we're heading back to Cheyenne."

The former drover looked at him. "You're giving up? Can't imagine that. They say you have never let a fugitive get away from you."

Crane knew of his own reputation all too well. If he had paper on a man, he found that man, and he either shot him or brought him in.

A dime novel had been written about Hannibal Crane. *The Tin Star: The Life and Times of Hannibal Crane, U.S. Marshal.* Mostly fiction, but it left a lot to live up to. People brought copies of the book to him for his autograph.

Part of the deal he had made when the writer interviewed him was that he got twenty percent of the royalties. If he hoped to continue business relationships of that sort in the future, he couldn't start letting outlaws get away from him.

And the man he was pursuing wasn't just any outlaw. He was Joe McCabe, the brother of Johnny McCabe. Crane could see a possible book about this very pursuit. Not that the pursuit had been glamorous or noteworthy so far, but that could be changed with the stroke of a pen.

"I'm not giving up on McCabe," Crane said to the drover. "But part of being as successful as I have been at hunting down fugitives is not wasting my time on wild goose chases. I'll find him. But I won't find him in these mountains, because I don't believe he's here. I doubt he ever was."

Supper was going to be what it had been every night since they had left Cheyenne. A can of beans dropped into a skillet and heated over a fire.

Crane had heard much about how wonderful food was when it was cooked outdoors, over a fire. He, for one, preferred to be indoors, under a roof, and to have food prepared in a fine restaurant.

As the beans heated and a kettle of coffee boiled, and daylight faded to twilight, Crane stood by the fire and thought about Joe McCabe.

McCabe was a wild man, so it was said. Spent time among the Indians and became something of a savage himself. Of what Crane had heard of the three McCabe brothers, Joe struck him as the least intelligent. Crane had never met him, but it was said he often spoke in grunts and growls, and he would take your scalp if you crossed him. What would motivate McCabe to spring the Compton woman from jail, Crane couldn't imagine. A woman found guilty of cutting her husband's throat while he slept. From what Crane had heard, Joe McCabe was half mad–he supposed a man like that needed no rational explanation for anything he did.

Then something occurred to Crane. There was one central feature in the entire McCabe legend. The McCabe Ranch in Montana. Could it be possible Joe would go there?

Crane thought the ranch might be a place to focus his search. It certainly beat wandering randomly through these mountains.

Come morning, he and his men would be starting back to the town of Cheyenne. Then, after a hot bath and one night in an actual bed, Marshal Crane would be catching a train for the town of Jubilee Montana. A town not far from the McCabe Ranch.

Joe McCabe, he thought, *I'm coming for you.*

PART THREE

The Valley

26

Late July, 1884

They rode across the valley. Josh, Dusty and Charles. They each wore chaps and were covered in dust and sweat, which turned the color of their clothing to a desert neutral.

"Three days out at the line shack," Charles said. "First thing I'm gonna do is climb into a hot bath."

Josh said, "I'm thinking the first thing I'm gonna do is pour a glass of scotch and wash down all the trail dust I've been eating for three days."

"I'll do you both one better," Dusty said. "I'm gonna sit in a hot bath *and* have a scotch. All at the same time."

Josh grinned. "I like the way you think. I knew we kept you around for a good reason."

They came to the wooden bridge, the shoes of their horses clattering along the wooden timbers. Dusty turned off toward the cabin he and Haley called home, and Josh and Charles continued on to the main house.

They reined up by the corral, and as Josh swung out of the saddle, he said, "You know, the thought of a hot bath is sounding better by the moment. I'm only twenty-seven, but I think I'm already getting too old to spend three straight days in the saddle. Every joint in my body hurts."

Charles said, "You still want us all to head to the mountains tomorrow for some mustanging?"

"I may want to re-think that. Maybe I was being overly ambitious."

Charles laughed.

Scott Hansen was in the corral. He said, "I'll take care of your horses, boys."

"I'll take you up on that," Josh said.

Josh and Charles walked up to the house, in the slow, tired way of men who have been in the saddle for three long days.

Josh said to Charles, "I figured you would have headed off to your and Bree's cabin."

Charles shook his head. "She's been staying with Pa and Jessica, while we were off at the line shack. I was thinking I might try to wrangle a supper invitation from you and Temperance."

Josh grinned. "Consider yourself invited."

They used the back door, stepping into the kitchen. Temperance was at the stove. Her hair was pulled back into a bun and she had a bandana over her hair like a kerchief.

She gave Josh a quick kiss.

He said, "I've been gone three days and that's all I get for a kiss?"

"Smelling that way," she said, "you're lucky you got any kind of a kiss at all."

Charles grinned.

Steak was frying in the skillet with onions. The steak was cut into small chunks. Temperance was stirring it all, swishing it around and flipping the steak chunks over. Oil was in the pan, sizzling away.

She said, "We're having something Mister Chen showed me how to cook."

"Sure does smell good," Josh said.

"Steak, onions, garlic and green peppers. He gave me the name for it, but I couldn't begin to pronounce it."

Josh looked over her shoulder at the skillet. "You got the meat already cut up."

She nodded. "It's the Chinese way. According to Mister Chen, if a dinner guest needs to use a knife to cut their food, the cook is insulted."

"I'd hate to have you feel insulted." He was smiling.

She gave him a look of mock annoyance. "I will be insulted if you come to the dinner table smelling like that."

Josh and Charles didn't have time for full baths before dinner, but when they joined Temperance at the table, they both smelled decidedly better. They had washed up and shaved, and were in clean shirts.

Josh chewed into a forkful of stir-fried steak. "Dang, but this is good."

Charles said, "I remember when I was growing up in New York, when I wandered to the Chinese neighborhoods, the smells of their cooking would make my mouth water."

"Oh," Temperance said, "we had a visitor this

afternoon. Marshal Crane. A U.S. Marshal."

Josh said, "What would a U.S. Marshal be doing out here?"

"He's looking for Uncle Joe."

Josh glanced at Charles. "Should'a figured something like this would happen, I suppose."

Charles nodded.

A few months ago, a reward poster had arrived at the Marshal's office in Jubilee. Their cousin Tom was the town marshal, and he rode out to the ranch to tell them about it.

Temperance said, "According to the marshal, everything is true. That woman really did kill her husband, and Uncle Joe broke her out of jail. He said he expects Uncle Joe to come here. The marshal said he'll be staying at the Randall Hotel in town, and if we have any contact with Uncle Joe, we're to report it to the marshal."

Josh took a bite of the stir-fry, letting himself enjoy the flavor, and letting everything Temperance had said roll itself around in his head.

He said to Charles, "I suppose we're gonna have to forget about mustanging. First thing in the morning, we'd better ride out to the canyon and get Pa."

27

The following morning, as the sun was beginning to show itself above the long ridge to the east of the ranch house, Josh and Charles saddled up and began the long ride across to the small canyon Pa and Jessica called home.

By noon, Josh and Pa were riding down the main street of Jubilee, toward the Randall Hotel.

They dismounted in front of the hotel. A man was standing on the porch in front of the hotel, with a smoldering cigar in one hand. He was in a gray three-piece suit and a bolo tie. His hair was a steel gray and he had a thick mustache and sideburns. Pinned to his vest was the shield of a U.S. Marshal.

"Johnny McCabe," the man said. "Your hair is longer than I remember, but otherwise you haven't changed all that much."

Johnny said, "You must be Marshal Crane. I've heard the name over the years, but I didn't realize we had met."

"A long time ago, briefly, back in Texas. You were with the Rangers, and I was a shotgun rider for a stagecoach company. A stage had been attacked and burned by Mexican raiders and you were one of the Rangers sent to investigate."

The memory came to life in Johnny's mind. He hadn't thought about those days in a long time.

He said, "Clarksville."

Crane nodded with a grin.

Johnny said, "I remember the incident, and the shotgun rider. I didn't remember the name, and I didn't realize that shotgun rider was the Hannibal Crane I've heard about over the years."

Crane gave the smile of a man trying to appear humble, but who liked the idea of his name being mentioned.

He said, "They do talk about me, I suppose. But, of course, you're here to talk about your brother."

"Aren't you?"

"Let's go inside and I'll buy you both a drink."

"Not here. The man who owns this hotel has caused a lot of problems for this family."

They headed across the street to the Second Chance. Crane ordered a whiskey for himself, and Hunter fetched two cold mugs of beer for the McCabes.

"Let's get to the point," Josh said.

Johnny said to Crane, "My son, Josh."

"Yes, indeed," Crane said. "I've heard you have three sons."

"Four, counting Eli. But we're here to talk about Joe."

Crane took a draw of smoke from his cigar. "He broke a woman out of jail, down in Cheyenne. A woman convicted of killing her husband. She did it in a rather grisly way, you see. She cut his throat while he lay sleeping in their bed. The cold-blooded heartlessness of it is why the prosecutor went for the death penalty."

"We haven't seen Joe for about a year," Johnny said. "But word has reached us."

The name Katrina Compton was given on the reward poster on the wall at Tom's office down the street, and it gave Johnny reason to reach back into his memory. The last name meant nothing to him at all, but the first name, when connected to Joe, rang some bells.

Johnny said, "Tell me more about the woman."

"She's an English woman. Married a man by the name of Elias Compton, also from England."

"How old is she?"

"How old? Thirty-nine, I believe. Her husband and his older brother became quite successful in business in Oregon, and were expanding into cattle and mining in Wyoming and Montana. They were considering buying into a mine outside of Jubilee."

Josh looked at his father. "Do any of those names sound familiar?"

Johnny said to Crane, "Her maiden name wouldn't be Waddell, would it?"

Crane said, "Why, yes."

"I'll be danged."

Josh said, "What is it, Pa?"

"I know that woman. Your Uncle Joe and I, and Zack, met her that summer when we first found the valley. She had been in a wagon train and was captured by

Indians. We rescued her and returned her to the wagons. But she and your Uncle Joe, they fell in love faster'n I have ever seen anyone fall in love. Well, except for maybe your mother and me."

Josh was looking at his father with wonder. "I never knew Uncle Joe was ever in love. It's kind'a hard to imagine."

"The problem was, she was engaged to be married to a farmer from England. A friend of her family."

"That Elias Compton fella."

Johnny nodded and glanced to the marshal. "I had forgotten his name, over the years. None of us ever saw her again."

Josh said, "Except now it looks like they've found each other again."

"This sounds like a wonderful love story," Crane said, "but none of it changes the fact that she killed her husband, and your brother broke her out of jail. Unless..."

The marshal's eyes were sparkling, the way a person's do when an idea occurs to them. "Unless they have indeed been in contact over the years, and she killed her husband so she and your brother could be together."

Johnny shook his head. "Not Joe."

"He broke her out of jail. A woman convicted of a grisly murder. What makes you think he couldn't have been part of the whole thing? Love is the one area, I've found, where people are most willing to cross the line."

"Not Joe."

Josh said to the marshal, "It's a McCabe thing."

Crane gave Josh a weary look. "And what, pray-tell, do you mean by that?"

Johnny said, "Honor and justice is a family tradition with us, going back at least to the first McCabe to come to this country. And probably back before that."

"Well, if you want to talk about justice, then why did he break that woman out of jail?"

"Because he probably didn't think she's guilty," Josh said. "And he's not going to let an innocent woman hang. Especially when he's in love with her."

"You see, Marshal," Johnny said, "in our family, we define the word *justice* as doing what's right. It's not right to let an innocent person hang."

Crane said, "And his opinion is more important than that of a jury?"

"I've met the woman. I find it very hard to believe she's capable of murder. She might be capable of killing— we all are if we're pushed hard enough. But outright cold-blooded murder?" Johnny shook his head. "No. Your jury is wrong. I don't know the particulars of the case, but I don't need to."

"What you're talking about is outright vigilantism."

Josh said, "If your back was to a wall and it was a life-and-death situation, believe me, my Uncle Joe is the kind of man you would want standing with you."

"I'm not talking about morality, or right and wrong. I'm talking about the law."

Johnny said, "Don't you find it sad that right and wrong, and the law, aren't always the same thing?"

"It's not my place to stand in judgment. I'm a lawman. My job is to bring your brother in. He'll have his say in front of a jury. They'll decide on the definition of justice."

Josh snickered. "If you can find him."

"What's that supposed to mean?"

Johnny said, "There's not a man alive who can see him if he doesn't want to be seen, or who can find him if he doesn't want to be found."

Josh laughed. It was an old family joke, something Joe had said more than once.

Josh said "Uncle Joe says it better."

Johnny shrugged. "He has that tight-lipped way of talking, and almost growling."

Josh said, keeping his lips tight and growling with his voice, "There ain't a man alive can find me if I don't want to be found."

Johnny laughed and nodded his head. "That's it."

Crane was not amused. He said, "I see nothing funny about any of this."

"We don't either. Not really."

"Let me assure you, Mister McCabe, your brother might think no one is capable of finding him, but I have always gotten my man. Like Bass Reeves and Heck Thomas. I have never let a fugitive escape."

"I've heard those names," Johnny said. "But they've

never tried to bring in my brother Joe."

"My record speaks for itself, and it will when I bring in your brother."

"I think we're done here."

"I expect him to show up in this area, eventually. Unless he's already here."

Josh said, "Do you really think we'd tell you?"

"I feel it's my duty to tell you that if you in any way assist him, you could be guilty of a crime. I'll have men watching your ranch. If he should show up there, he'll be arrested."

"Understand this," Johnny said. "No man has ever been taken off our ranch."

"Do you know what kind of trouble you're bringing down on yourself?"

Johnny was no longer grinning. He was deadly serious. "Do you know what kind of trouble *you*'ll be bringing down on *your*self?"

Josh said, "I'm going to give you fair warning about trespassing. Stay off McCabe land. If we see you or anyone working for you on our land, we'll shoot you on sight."

"I can get a warrant."

"Keep in mind," Johnny said, "this is remote country. It's still the frontier in a lot of ways. I'll put a bullet against your warrant, any day."

Johnny downed the last of his beer. Josh had already finished his.

"Nice talking to you, Crane," Johnny said. "But I hope we don't have to see you again."

Josh got to his feet. "Do yourself a favor. Go back to where you came from."

Josh and his father walked across the barroom floor and out into the street.

Crane's glass was empty so he waved Hunter over and asked for a refill. Hunter pulled the cork from the bottle and dumped two ounces of whiskey into Crane's glass.

Hunter said, "If you don't mind some friendly advice..."

"Actually, I do mind."

Hunter continued anyway. "I'd forget about Joe McCabe. You'll never take him in. I doubt you'll ever even find him."

"No man is above the law."

"I'm sure you've heard the stories about the McCabes."

"What man hasn't?"

"I've known both Johnny and Joe for a long time. The stories—they're all true. At least, most of 'em. I wouldn't want to ride down on Johnny McCabe or his sons even if I had a whole army of deputies with me. And I sure wouldn't want to give Joe reason to kill me."

Hunter set the bottle on a shelf behind the bar. "And let me tell you something else. If Joe McCabe rescued that gal from the gallows, there had to be good reason. I'd bet my life on the judgment of Joe and Johnny."

Crane said, "It's not about judgment. It's about the law, and which side of it you stand on."

"Actually," Hunter said, "it's about who will pay for your funeral."

28

Johnny stepped out of the cabin, and he had his tin cup filled with coffee. The eastern horizon was only beginning to show the light of morning. Inside, Jessica had bacon sizzling away in a frying pan, and she was fixing hot cakes.

Johnny had been greeting the day with a cup of coffee for a lot of years, but breakfast smelled so good he planned to cut his morning's greeting short.

He had built a fence at the edge of the little shelf where he had built the cabin. In some ways, this canyon was similar to the one in California where Jessica and Cora had lived. This one was smaller, though. The canyon in California could accommodate a couple hundred head of cattle. This one could handle no more than the small remuda Johnny kept on hand.

In the gray light of early morning, Johnny could see the canyon floor, down below. Thunder was galloping about, his mane flowing in the morning breeze. The horse reared up, kicking his hooves in the air. Then he turned and ran off to the far side of the canyon, beyond Johnny's view.

One longhorn was down there, grazing lazily on the grass that grew thick and green on the canyon floor. Old Blue, the steer that had led the herd on many a trail drive. He seemed to be enjoying his retirement.

Johnny felt motion to one side, and he glanced over. A wolf was standing thirty feet from him.

He heard Joe's voice. "Don't worry. He's a friend."

Joe was standing by the corner of the house. His hair was longer than ever.

"So," Johnny said. "You're commanding the wild beasts, now?"

Joe shook his head. "This one comes and goes as he pleases."

"Like someone else I know."

Joe walked up to Johnny and shook his hand, and then they hugged. Johnny's coffee dumped to the ground but he didn't care.

Johnny said "I'm not surprised to see you. There's a man in town looking for you."

"A U.S. Marshal?"

Johnny nodded.

Joe said, "He got here fast."

"Let's go in and grab some coffee. Sounds like you have a story to tell."

Joe nodded. "I do. But first, I want you to meet someone you haven't seen in a lot of years."

Joe looked back to a line of short pines between the ranch house and the canyon wall. A rider came through the trees, leading a second horse. How Joe and the rider could have gotten into the canyon and behind the house without Johnny being aware of it, Johnny wasn't going to bother asking.

The rider was a woman. She drew closer, and in the gray morning light, Johnny realized he was looking at a face he indeed hadn't seen in many a year.

"Kate Waddell," he said.

She was smiling. "Johnny. It's so good to see you, again."

"You haven't changed a bit, except that you're dressed like a Cheyenne."

They left the horses at a hitching rail in front of the house. When they stepped into the cabin, Cora screamed out, "Uncle Joe!" And she ran to him and he scooped her up in a hug.

"Girl," he said, "you've grown two inches."

Eli was there, and he extended his hand, and said, "Uncle Joe."

Eli's voice had dropped a little in pitch over the past year that Joe had been away, and Eli was not only taller, but he had filled out his shirt with muscle.

"You were still a boy when I left," Joe said, "but now you're a man."

Hugs were given all around, and Joe introduced everyone to Kate.

Eli said, "I'll go take care of the horses."

Johnny laid a hand on his shoulder. "I have another job for you."

They stepped out onto the front porch.

Johnny said, "I want you to saddle a horse and go get your brothers. And be fast about it."

Johnny saw that Eli was wearing a gunbelt. Johnny said, "And grab a rifle. While you ride, watch for any tracks of riders. And be careful."

"I will, Pa."

Joe had followed them outside. He said, "No one saw us ride in. I'm sure of that."

"So am I," Johnny said. "But the impression I have is Marshal Crane is no fool. If we let ourselves get careless around him, we won't get any second chances."

29

By early afternoon, Eli was returning with Dusty and Josh. Matt was with them.

Eli said to Pa, "I took it onto myself to go get Uncle Matt."

Johnny nodded. "Good thinking, son."

That evening, with a fire going in the hearth, Kate sat in a rocker. She had enjoyed the luxury of a hot bath, which she figured would probably be her last for a while. She was now in a fresh buckskin dress.

"I love that dress," M.J. said.

"Thank you. Joe showed me how to make it. It's the way Cheyenne women dress."

She looked at Johnny and said, "The years have been kind to both you and Joe. Your hair is longer than I remember. Joe told me about the winter you all spent with the Shoshone. I hope Zack Johnson is well."

Johnny nodded. "He has a ranch at this side of the valley. He's married and has a family."

Johnny was in the chair he had made years ago, with a frame of narrow wooden timbers and with cowhide stretched across the seat and back. Johnny had brought it with him from the main ranch house.

Kate said, "Seeing you and Joe together brings back those days, when I was captured by that horrible Indian and you all rescued me. It was so long ago, but at the moment, it seems like just yesterday."

She talked about how she had married Elias Compton. "It was an arrangement we had back in England, when we were very young. I thought I knew what love was, but what we had was really little more than friendship and convenience. I saw that, once I met Joe. That was when I found that I hadn't known what love was at all. I returned to Elias because I had promised to marry him, but over the years, I wondered if I had done the right thing."

Joe was standing by the hearth, leaning a hand on a timber that served as a mantel. He said, "You don't have to talk about all of that, if'n you don't want to."

"Yes, I think I need to. I think if we're going to pull everyone into this, they have a right to know."

Matt said, "Actually, just that Joe believes in you and is happy with you is enough for us. He's always had good judgment."

Joe looked at him with surprise. "I don't think I've ever heard you admit that."

Matt was smiling. "It won't happen again, either."

Johnny was grinning. He had a glass of scotch in one hand. He said, "It's so good having the three of us together again."

Matt nodded. "It truly is."

Joe said, "It may not happen again, for a while. Kate and I have some riding to do. We have to outrun the reach of the law."

Jessica said to Kate, "Is there any way to prove that

you didn't kill Elias? Or to find out who did?"

Kate shrugged. "I don't see how."

Joe said, "If we could go back to Cheyenne and ask the right questions. Jack has a good mind for that sort of thing. I bet he could get to the bottom of it all. But we can't do it if we have the law on our tail."

Kate said, "The real tragedy in all of this is what happened to Elias. He was a good man. The love we thought we had just wasn't there. He was honest and a good businessman. His brother, Jonah, however was a different sort. Even back in England, there was something dark about him. Something that made you feel you didn't want to turn your back on him."

She had a cup of tea in her hands, and she took a sip.

She said, "They went into business together, and Jonah had a good head for business. I'll say that for him. They expanded into lumber and cattle. I accompanied them on business trips, every so often. I went along on the business trip to Cheyenne, which was the last one Elias would ever make."

"What happened?" Matt said.

"One evening, we had an argument. I forget what it was about. When you're in a marriage with no love, stupid arguments happen. I suppose it's the result of the loneliness we both felt. He went to bed and I sat up in my room to read. We had rented a house in Cheyenne, and my room had a hearth. I sat up, reading by the fire. I fell asleep. When I eventually woke up, the fire had burned down. I must have been asleep for at least an hour. Elias and I had separate bedrooms—we had for years. I noticed his door was ajar, which was odd. He usually kept his door shut. And his light was still on. I stepped in to make sure everything was all right, and I found him dead."

She gave a little shudder. "His throat was cut. There was blood everywhere. I screamed and ran from the house. I found the marshal, a man named Kincaid."

Johnny nodded. "I've met him before."

"They found a bloody knife in my bedroom, so Marshal Kincaid had to arrest me. I don't think he really believed I did it, but Jonah seemed to believe it all too willingly, and the prosecutor went after me with a vengeance."

Joe said, "Someone got into the house while you were sleeping and done it."

Johnny was watching the way she moved when she spoke. The tone of her voice. He had known murderers over the years, and he was asking himself if she could have actually done it. If she could have cut her husband's throat. He wanted to believe her, and he knew Joe already did, but sometimes wanting wasn't enough.

He glanced at Jessica, who had crossed a few hills in her time and seen some of the bad things life has to offer. It would take a lot to fool her. Her eyes were on Kate. Johnny knew Jess well enough to understand by the way she sat, the look in her eyes, that Jess believed her.

Johnny had a question to ask, but he didn't know

how to do it without seeming impolite. He decided to just ask it.

"Did Marshal Kincaid arrest you immediately, or did he let you change your clothes, first?"

Kate looked at him with a question in her eyes, like a woman who didn't want to seem impolite but who didn't understand the question.

Matt was holding back a grin, but his eyes were crinkling at the corners. Johnny figured Matt knew the line of questioning he was pursuing.

Johnny said to Kate, "All of the blood. On your clothes."

She blinked with surprise. "There was no blood on my clothes. I didn't get close enough to Elias to get his blood on me."

Johnny looked at Joe. Kate looked from Johnny to Joe, and she said, "I have to admit I'm confused."

Joe said, "When a man's throat is cut, blood sprays. It can spray across the room for a few seconds. If Elias had been layin' in bed and you cut his throat, you would have been covered in his blood."

Kate looked at Johnny.

Joe said, "Johnny was asking you the way he did to make sure you didn't do it." He looked at Johnny. "And I gotta say, I don't appreciate it."

"No," Kate said, "it's all right. I fully understand. I would have done the same. Everyone here is being asked to accept a lot on simply my word and no more."

"I still don't like it," Joe said.

Johnny nodded to his brother. "Should I apologize?"

Kate said, "Absolutely not. Here we come, barging in on you like this, putting you all at risk and asking you to accept my word alone that I didn't do the crime I'm accused of."

Joe said, "I believe her. I know her better'n any of you. I seen a lot, and I know a killer when I see one. If you can't accept her word, then you should accept mine. You know me. I'm your brother. I grew up with you in Ma and Pa's old farm house in Pennsylvania, and we crossed the country together. I killed the man what killed Lura, just so you wouldn't have to face a noose."

Johnny nodded. "You're right. I'm sorry. I was out of line."

Matt said, "Joe, put yourself in our place. If Johnny or I had ridden in, like you and Kate did. What would you think?"

Joe was about to say something, then held it back. He looked at Kate, then back at Matt. "I don't know. Maybe you got a point."

Jessica said, "Who do you think did it?"

Josh was standing by the hearth. He said, "Jack has talked a lot about this kind of thing. He said you always have to look for motive. Who would have benefited most by his death."

"Me, I suppose," Kate said, "because now I'm with Joe. I couldn't have been, before."

Johnny said, "But you couldn't have known that Joe would ride into town and rescue you from the gallows. Is there someone else who could benefit from it?"

She shrugged. "I can't imagine. Since we were in separate bedrooms the prosecutor claimed I was a lonely woman trapped in a loveless marriage and killed to get my freedom. It was all very lurid, and the jury loved it."

"That's nonsense," Jessica said. "I didn't always have the life I have now. There was a time when I met people from different walks of life. Johnny has said before that everyone is capable of killing, if they're pushed far enough, but I've known more than one person in a loveless marriage, and by itself that's not enough to push someone to kill."

Matt said, "Was there any financial gain you would have from his death?"

Kate shrugged again. "Not that I can imagine. He and I were owners of half of the businesses he owned with his brother. After his death, I would continue to own half of those assets. There was nothing else to gain."

"There are no heirs?"

Joe said, "She and I already talked about all of this."

Kate took a sip of tea. "Elias and I had no children. His half would remain solely in my name."

"I hate to ask this. What would have happened if the hanging had been carried out?"

"Then ownership of the businesses would all go to Jonah."

Joe said, "Kate and me already talked this through, and we came around to that line of thinking"

Kate nodded. "With me gone, he would have sole ownership of all of the businesses he and Elias built or bought into. Overall, it's a sizable amount of money."

Matt nodded his head toward Johnny, as if to say, *What do you think?*

Johnny said, "If I was investigating that murder, Jonah Compton is where I would start."

"Joe and I talked about it, and I've done a lot of thinking about it since," Kate said, "I have to admit, Jonah is no one I would really trust. But to murder his own brother? I would hope he's not capable of that sort of thing."

Joe said, "We'll likely never know who did it. The only way would be to go back, and we ain't doing that. I ain't gonna risk them hanging Kate."

Johnny nodded, "I don't think you'll get an argument from anyone here."

"So," Josh said to Joe, "what's your plan?"

Joe said, "We're heading for Canada. I remember a nice stretch of mountains, back when we were hiding Sam, just after we broke him out of prison."

Dusty nodded. "The Bow River valley. That sure was remote country. Not a town for a hundred miles or more."

"We'll build a cabin and live off the land. I'll run a trap line, because we'll need supplies, now and then. The town of Calgary is a three or four day ride from the place I have in mind."

Johnny said, "The winters are long that far north, and hard."

Kate smiled. "I'm of hardy stock."

"Ma'am, of that I have no doubt."

Joe said, "We're gonna need a load of supplies up front. I don't know how to get 'em in town, if that marshal is still there. And I don't have any cash left."

"I have assets," Kate said, "but that money was frozen pending the outcome of the trial. I would have no way of getting to a bank and making a withdrawal, anyway."

Johnny said, "We'll get you those supplies. Don't worry about the money."

"We'll need two pack horses, too," Joe said. "I don't normally travel with enough supplies to need a pack horse, but this is different."

"We'll get you those pack horses," Josh said. "You can have your choice of any horses in the remuda."

"We don't want charity. Even from family."

"Joe," Jessica said, "it's not charity when family helps each other."

"Much obliged. But what about the marshal?"

Johnny said, "I have an idea how to handle him."

As Johnny started telling them his idea, Dusty noticed Eli had stepped out. Dusty went to the kitchen expecting to find Eli at the coffee kettle. Eli was now working for Josh on the ranch, and like every cowhand Dusty had ever met, Eli had developed a taste for coffee. But Eli wasn't in the kitchen.

Then Dusty figured out where Eli had probably gone. Dusty stepped out onto the porch. The night had turned chilly but he was in his buckskin shirt which was as warm as any jacket.

The moon was at three quarters, and it gave enough light that he could see the canyon down below. The small remuda Pa kept here at the canyon appeared as nothing but dark shapes below, but all seemed quiet.

Dusty reached to his pistol and loosened it in the holster, just to be ready. He didn't expect anything was wrong, and he was not as jumpy as Pa, but it was good to be cautious.

The small shelf that held the cabin wound its way down toward the canyon floor. The canyon was open at one end only, and even then, the opening was narrow. Two riders could come through, side-by-side, as long as there wasn't too much daylight between them.

Dusty found Eli at the canyon opening. Eli had taken a Winchester from Pa's rifle rack.

Dusty said, "I thought I'd find you down here."

"I just got to thinking that maybe we should watch the canyon opening, but I didn't want to say anything and scare Ma, Missy or Miss Kate."

"M.J. hates it when you call her Missy. But you

know that."

Eli grinned. "Yeah."

Eli was in a shirt that looked to be a neutral gray in the darkness, but in daylight was a chestnut brown. He wore jeans, and at his right side was a gun. Pa and Dusty had both been working with him on his draw and his marksmanship. Eli was a quick study.

Dusty said, "You're a good man to have around, you know that?"

Eli smiled. "It means a lot for you to say that."

"You and I have something in common. The McCabe name isn't something we were born into. And yet it's ours now, as much as anyone's."

Dusty had told Eli of his background. Raised by outlaws and not learning the name of his father until he was twenty years old.

Eli said, "Where do you think you'd be right now if you had never learned you were a McCabe?"

Dusty shrugged. "Probably would have gone back to Arizona, to the Cantrell Ranch. I still have the horse Mister Cantrell gave me. He told me if I didn't find what I was looking for, that I would always have a job waiting for me."

"I'd probably still be at that old, rickety cabin in Idaho. Me and Missy."

They heard the sound of a stone skittering on the dirt, from just outside the canyon entrance. Something had moved out there and it had kicked a rock as it did so.

Dust drew his pistol and motioned for Eli to fall into place behind him. They held to the rock wall of the canyon entrance and made their way along.

Then something moved in front of them. It was low to the ground and walking toward them.

An animal, Dusty could see. He held his pistol ready and cocked the hammer. Behind him, Eli jacked a round into his rifle's chamber.

The animal stepped closer and Dusty saw what it was. He chuckled.

"Hold your fire," he said. "It's Uncle Joe's wolf."

Poe stepped closer and stood in the moonlight. He was looking at them and his tail was wagging.

"Poe," Eli said, "you gotta be careful out here, or you're gonna get yourself shot."

Dusty released the hammer of his revolver and slid the gun back into his holster.

Eli said, "Why do you suppose Uncle Joe took a wolf as a pet?"

Dusty shrugged his shoulders. "From what he said, the wolf chose him."

30

The next morning, Johnny rode along the main street of Jubilee. He was on a bay gelding. He still rode Thunder occasionally, now that Thunder's hoof had healed, but the horse was getting older and Johnny thought the old boy had earned some leisure time.

Johnny saw Marshal Crane standing in front of the hotel, a cigar in one hand. Johnny reined up in front of him.

Crane said, "Well, McCabe. In town two days in a row, I see."

Johnny nodded his head. "Your powers of observation are astounding."

Crane laughed.

Johnny said, "I was hoping to find you had hopped the train for points south."

"I'm not going anywhere, until your brother and that woman are in handcuffs."

Johnny grinned. "You may have a long time to wait."

Crane took a draw from his cigar and let the smoke out through a grin. "I'm starting to think you're buying into too much of your legend. You're not big enough to stand against the federal government."

"I'll always stand for the rights of one man or woman against a bully. Even a bully who is using the federal government as his source of power."

Crane gave him a long look. "They call you a gunhawk, but you know what you are? You're a crusader. And you know what happens to crusaders? They wind up being looked at as heroes, but they also wind up dying young. You get my meaning?"

Johnny's horse was getting a little restless. It lifted a hoof and set it back down, and swished its tail at a horsefly.

Johnny said to Crane, "It sounds like you're threatening me."

Crane shook his head. "Just a good neighborly warning."

It was Johnny's turn to give Crane a long look. Johnny said, "You're treading in dangerous territory. Just so you know that."

"As long as you know you're doing the same."

Johnny decided enough had been said here, and he turned his horse toward the Second Chance. The horse was more than happy to get moving.

Johnny left the horse at the hitching rail, which was in the shade at the front of the Second Chance. There was a small breeze coming from the ridge that rose behind the Second Chance, and the breeze would keep horseflies away.

Johnny found Hunter behind the bar, fitting a tap to a keg of beer. Mr. Chen was working the barroom floor with a broom.

Johnny brought them both up to date on Joe's situation. By the time he was finished, Hunter was done with the beer tap and was leaning with both elbows on the bar. Chen had stopped sweeping and was leaning on his broom.

Johnny said, "I need a favor from both of you."

Hunter glanced at Chen and said, "I'll do anything to help Joe."

Chen nodded. "Without question."

Johnny grinned. "I was hoping you would both say that."

Johnny mounted up but instead of taking the main trail back into the valley, he cut around the Second Chance and to the line of trees out back. He seldom took this trail anymore, because it came out at the ranch itself. When he left town these days, he usually took the main trail to the valley, then across the valley and out to the little canyon where he and Jessica now made their home.

The trail that began behind the Second Chance wound its way between rocks and around stands of trees. Through a ravine and up a small incline. It cut through a thickly wooded ravine, and was impassible in the winter and spring.

Johnny rode for about half a mile, then he turned his horse away from the trail and into a stand of pines that grew short and thick. There he waited.

He didn't have to wait long before a horse came into

view along his back trail. It was Crane. Johnny waited until Crane was past the line of pines, then rode out behind him.

Crane reined up and turned around in the saddle. He said, "You think you're funny, don't you?"

Johnny pulled up beside him. "A little."

"Well, you're not."

"You like to live dangerously, don't you?"

"You threatening me?"

Johnny shrugged his shoulders. "Just making an observation."

"You know, McCabe, it's just the two of us out here. No witnesses. If I claim you drew on me, it would be my word against that of a dead man in court."

"You really gonna draw on me? More than one man has, and yet here I am. They're all in the ground."

"I don't believe half of those stories people tell about you."

"The question is, which half should you believe?"

Crane looked at him, squinting his eyes a little in the sun. Then he took the cigar out of his mouth, flicked some ash, and he said, "All right, McCabe. You've won this round. But it's not over."

"I couldn't be so lucky."

"I'm going to ride away. I trust you won't shoot me in the back."

"I've never shot a man in the back. Never will."

Crane nodded, returned the cigar to his mouth and

then turned his horse around.

Johnny said, "You're not going to win this battle. You might think you will, because you've never lost. But you won't win this one."

Crane looked over his shoulder at him. "What makes you so sure?"

"Between my brothers and me, I'm the one with the reputation, for some reason. The one everyone's heard of. But Joe's the one you don't want mad at you. Besides, like I said before, if he broke that woman out of jail, you can bet there's a good reason. Ride on, Marshal, and chase down some real criminals."

Crane turned his horse back around so he could face Johnny. "Your brother is the real criminal, McCabe. This is not the frontier any longer. Civilization is coming, and with civilization comes law. Laws we all have to obey. There's no place in civilization for a wild man who has no respect for the law."

Johnny nodded his head. "Civilization is coming, but it's not here yet. This is a wild land, and it takes hard men to live here. Ride on, Marshal. You'll never take my brother alive.

"I'd be just as satisfied to take him draped over a saddle."

"What I mean is *you* won't be alive."

Johnny began to turn his horse toward the valley. He said, "Don't follow me, Marshal. This is my land and trespassers will be shot on sight, badge or not. Don't test me."

Crane sat in the saddle and watched Johnny ride on. He took a draw on his cigar, and he turned his horse back toward town.

31

Joe glanced up at the moon and knew it was after midnight.

Behind him was the log ranch house that served as the headquarters to the McCabe Ranch. He paced from the house to the barn and out beyond it, then returned to the house. At the moment, he was standing in front of the front porch, his scattergun tucked in the crook of one arm.

Joe was normally a patient man. You can't live in the wilderness if you weren't patient. Hunting, trapping and growing your own food were often slow processes. But tonight he felt impatience shooting through him.

Johnny, Matt and the boys had gone into town to load up a buckboard with supplies. Enough to last Kate and Joe a while. And Joe was able to do nothing but wait for them.

He had wanted to go along, but Johnny said, "Absolutely not." Even though it was the middle of the night, there was a chance that Marshal Crane could discover what they were up to. Johnny said he had a contingency plan in mind, but for it all to work, Joe had to wait at the house. If Crane were to find concrete proof that Joe was in the area, then he and Matt and the boys could be potentially brought up on charges. Johnny intended to help Joe and Kate, but without disrupting the lives of the family.

Contingency plan, Joe almost scoffed. A ten-dollar word. Johnny had been hanging around Matt too long. Picking up some bad habits.

Crickets chirped, and from out somewhere in the trees beyond the tangle of bushes beyond the eastern end of the ranch house, a hoot owl called out.

He paced about. He listened to the night for anything that sounded out of place.

At one point, he heard the sound of something brushing against a bush, and looked over in that direction to see Poe walking out of the tangle.

The wolf stopped at his side, and looked around.

Joe said, "We got us a long ride ahead of us, all the way to the Bow River valley. It ain't gonna be easy. And once we're there, we gotta get a cabin up before the first snow."

The wolf looked up at him, and then looked back out into the night.

At one point, Poe perked up his ears and stared at something in the darkness. Joe brought his scattergun up, in case he was going to need it. But then Poe gave up on whatever it was, his ears relaxed and he went back to glancing idly about.

Joe decided maybe a cup of coffee was in order. He walked around to the side of the house and used the kitchen door so he wouldn't wake anyone up. Kate was asleep in the parlor, on the sofa. Jessica and the girls were here, from the cabin out in the canyon. The infant twins were here, too. Not so much infants anymore, though. Joe had been gone a year, and the little ones were walking, now.

Joe said to Poe, "You stay out there, pup. I'll be right back."

He opened the door as carefully as he could. The hinge squealed. Johnny had always kept the hinges so they squealed, and he would know if a door was being opened at night. Now that Josh was the man of the house, he was apparently keeping up his father's practices.

Joe filled the coffee cup, then went back out into the night.

He walked back around to the front of the house, and climbed the steps of the porch. He leaned his scattergun against the porch railing and took a sip of his coffee.

The door opened behind him, and Kate stepped out.

Joe said, "You should be sleeping. Johnny and the boys will be back with the wagon in an hour or so, and we'll have to be on our way."

"I can't sleep," she said. "I tried, but it's hard to when there is so much going on. I heard you come into the kitchen and decided trying to sleep would be futile."

He nodded. "I'm filled with restlessness, myself. I ain't used to letting others fight my battles."

"Do you think there will be one? A battle, in town?"

He shrugged his shoulders. "They're going in late at night, when the town should be asleep. Hopefully the marshal will be, too. They shouldn't make a lot of noise, and they shouldn't be seen. They'll be filling the wagon from the backdoor of Franklin's. But you never know."

She had a shawl wrapped about her shoulders, to hold off the cold of the Montana night, but she still looked cold. He reached one arm around her shoulders and pulled her in for a hug.

"I feel so badly," she said, "bringing such hardships to your family. I've disrupted all of their lives."

Joe shook his head. "I'd do the same for them. That's what we do in this family. Help each other out, no matter what the cost."

"Since I'm awake, I think I'm going to go make some more coffee for you, and put on some tea water for me."

He nodded. "I'll be out here."

"Be careful."

He nodded again. "Poe's out here, somewhere, too. He and I'll take care of things."

Joe took another sip of coffee.

He shifted the cup to his left hand, and then flexed his right a couple of times. The hand he had taken the bullet in, back in Wardtown. Not just taken a bullet, but the bullet had gone clean through. Broke one bone, and cut nerves. Not that Joe knew quite what a nerve was, but the horse doctor that had patched him up used the term.

He had full motion of all of his fingers, though his middle finger was numb. But the hand didn't have the strength to handle a revolver. He couldn't hold it steady while he pulled the trigger, and the recoil would almost yank the gun right out of his hand. Not that he had ever been the expert with a pistol that Johnny was, or Dusty.

The door opened again and he expected it would be Kate, but it was M.J.

He said, "Emmy, why ain't you asleep?"

"How can I sleep? This could be the last night we see you for a long time. Maybe years."

She was in a night gown and had a blanket wrapped around her.

She said, "Jessica is asleep upstairs. Or at least, she's trying to sleep. She has the twins with her. Cora's in the kitchen with Aunt Ginny and Peddie and Kate."

Joe blinked with surprise. "They're all awake?"

M.J. nodded. "None of us can sleep. Temperance is in the parlor, starting a fire going."

"I feel bad, costing you all a night's sleep."

She shook her head. "Don't feel bad. We're all family. Sometimes family costs you a little sleep, but it's a sacrifice worth making. My father said that once, years ago, back in Virginia."

"Sounds like your father was a wise man."

Poe came walking into view, coming from behind the barn.

She said, "Hi, Poe."

She walked down the steps toward him.

"Careful, honey," Joe said. "That's a wild animal."

But she knelt down and the wolf came over to her.

"No he's not," she said, in the baby-talk sort of way so many women take on around animals, and she began scratching his head. "He's just a big baby. That's what he is."

She scratched at both sides of his neck, and then he dropped to the ground and rolled over so she could scratch his belly.

Joe said, "I forget how you are with animals. I'd swear, you could tame a grizzly."

"Just give me a chance and I will."

Joe chuckled. He knew she was joking, but if anyone could tame a bear, it would be her.

He said, "Could've used you back in the Big Horns about six months ago, when I got these scars on my face."

She said to the wolf, "You take care of Uncle Joe and Kate, now. Okay?"

Joe said, "Among the Cheyenne, you'd be considered a spirit woman. One who can communicate with the animals."

Bree came out onto the porch, a revolver holstered at her side and a Winchester in one hand.

She said, "I figured I'd keep watch with you, Uncle Joe."

He nodded. "Another gun is always welcome."

Aunt Ginny and Kate were behind her. Kate had a fresh cup of coffee for Joe, and they each had a cup of tea.

"We have such a big family now," Ginny said.

"Such a houseful, when we all come together here."

Joe said, "Weren't always that way."

She shook her head. "It surely wasn't. Do you remember when we first came to this valley?"

"Cain't hardly forget it."

"It seems like a lifetime ago. So much has changed. And yet, it also seems like just yesterday."

"I helped build this house."

"Yes you did."

"And now I'll be going away. Don't know how long we'll be gone. Maybe someday Kate and I can come back, but it won't be for a long time."

Ginny took a cup of tea. "Will you both be all right? I mean, from what you've been saying about that Bow River country, it sounds even more remote than this valley was when we first moved here."

Joe nodded. "We'll be fine. Kate has been learning fast. She's practically an Indian herself, now."

Kate chuckled. "I wouldn't quite say that."

After a time, they could see motion out beyond the covered bridge. Poe looked off in that direction. Then they heard the clatter of wagon wheels and horse hooves on the bridge.

"Here they come," Joe said.

The wagon came into view as it followed the trail up around the barn and toward the house. Josh was in the wagon seat. Four riders had gone to town with him. Johnny, Dusty, Matt and Eli. Five were returning, and Joe realized the fourth rider was Jack.

They pulled up in front of the porch.

Jack said, "I couldn't let you leave without saying goodbye."

Joe said to Johnny, "Everything go okay?"

Johnny swung out of the saddle. "Everything went without a hitch. Mister Chen was positioned at the hotel in case the marshal figured out what we were up to, but according to Chen he stayed in his room the whole time."

Ginny said, "Do I want to ask what Mister Chen would have done if the marshal figured it out?"

Johnny said, "No."

The men began transferring the supplies from the wagon to four pack horses, and horses were saddled for Joe and Kate.

Joe said, "I'll owe you for them horses."

Josh shook his head. "We're family. We take care of each other."

It was time for the goodbyes. Hugs and handshakes went all around. Tears were flowing.

Johnny said to Joe, "You got about three hours before sunrise."

Joe nodded. "Time for us to get moving. We should be well out of the valley by then."

Matt said, "You want us to ride with you part of the way? To make sure you get safely on your way?"

Joe shook his head. "Thanks for the offer, but the more horses, the more tracks we'll make. That marshal is apparently a good tracker."

Matt pulled Joe in for a hug.

Joe said, "You save some of them ten-dollar words for the next time I see you."

Matt nodded. "And we will see you again. That's a promise."

Joe held Kate's rein while she swung up and into the saddle. Not that she couldn't have mounted unassisted. She now rode a horse like she had been born to it. Then he mounted his own horse and took the reins of the pack team.

Joe looked at them all, wanting to cement each of them in his memory. He had said it would be a long time before he saw them again, but he knew in reality he might never see them again. His gaze finally settled on Johnny and Matt. They were standing side-by-side.

Joe said, "We come a long way together. From Pennsylvania to Texas. Then from there to that little valley in Colorado, then all the way to California. Then Johnny, you and me made the ride from California cross country to this valley. Twice. Then we done it with Matt again, a few years ago. I'm proud to have you both as brothers."

Matt said, "I hope you know the feeling is mutual."

"Yeah, I do," Joe nodded. "That's part of bein' family."

He and Kate turned their horses down toward the covered bridge.

Kate rode ahead of Joe. Josh had given her a

Winchester from the gun rack in the house, and she rode with it across the front of her saddle. Joe followed, leading the pack horses.

Jessica and Cora walked over to Johnny. Cora was now too tall and heavy for Johnny to heft onto his shoulder, so instead he took her hand.

Ginny wandered over. "Do you ever think we'll see them again?"

Johnny gave a shrug. He didn't quite know how to answer, so he didn't.

They stood and watched until Joe and Kate were past the covered bridge, and lost in the darkness.

32

Marshal Crane decided to take his morning coffee at the Second Chance. Many of the locals still did. The restaurant wasn't actually open until mid-morning, and the saloon half of the building until mid-afternoon, but the doors were open to some of the locals who would wander in. He had noticed Jack McCabe, the lawyer son of the gunfighter, often had coffee at the Second Chance. Jack's wife had joined him on one of the three mornings since Crane had arrived. The town marshal, also a McCabe, had coffee at the Second Chance every morning, and twice the local school marm had joined him.

Crane observed some of this himself, and the rest he obtained by asking the proper questions.

When he walked into the saloon half of the building, where the morning coffee was served, he received the reaction he had expected. People at tables turned to stare at him.

Marshal Tom McCabe was there, this time minus the school marm. Jack McCabe and his wife were at the same table. With them was a tall man with a thick beard. He looked to be maybe fifty, and if Crane were to bet dollars to doughnuts, it was the old outlaw Harlan Carter. From what Crane understood, Carter had disappeared years ago and most lawmen figured he was dead. Carter was wanted on at least fifteen counts of murder and even more counts of robbery, if Crane's memory was correct. He wondered what kind of reward might still be on Carter's head.

But Crane wasn't here to bring in Carter. He was here for Joe McCabe and Kate Compton. Once they were both behind bars, he might turn his attention to Carter.

The man behind the bar known as Hunter said, "We ain't actually open for business. This is just a get-together of town locals."

Jack said, "That's all right, Hunter. We can consider him our guest for today."

Hunter gave Jack a long look, and he grabbed a tin cup and filled it from one of two kettle's he had on the stove. He handed the cup to Crane.

The marshal went over to Jack's table, and Jack waved one hand toward an empty chair. The marshal slid the chair out and dropped into it.

He said, "I must admit, I'm a little surprised at the invitation. Or, is it a case of keeping your enemy close?"

Jack smiled but said nothing.

Crane said, "We haven't formally met."

"I know who you are," Jack said, "and I'm sure you know who I am."

"I know who everyone here is." He shot a quick glance at the man he believed to be Harlan Carter. The man was openly glaring at him.

Carter said, "If you got something to say, just say it."

Tom McCabe held up a hand. "Let's keep it civil, gentleman."

He glanced at Crane and said, "You might be a federal officer, but keeping the peace in this town is my job."

Crane nodded to him. "Point taken."

Carter continued to stare at Crane. He took a sip of his coffee, but didn't take his eyes from the lawman.

Crane figured if this was truly Harlan Carter, and if everything Crane had heard about him was true, the man probably wouldn't be well-versed in subtleties.

"So," Jack said. "Apparently you're staying in town for a while?"

Crane nodded. "Until I get my man. In this case, the man and the woman."

Crane took a sip of coffee, and he said, "I feel I would be remiss in my duties if I didn't point out there is such a thing as obstructing justice. If any of you in any way assist them in escaping the law, you could be brought up on charges of aiding and abetting."

Jack said, "You're explaining the law to an attorney and a town marshal."

Crane smiled and nodded. "Point taken, again."

Crane took another sip of his coffee. "I hope you know, I have nothing personal against your uncle. I'm just doing my job."

"What if he ain't guilty?" Carter said. "Or what if he had a good reason?"

Carter spoke through clenched teeth, with tight lips. Since no one around him reacted, Crane had to wonder if he always spoke that way.

Crane said, "It's not my job to play judge and jury. That's the job of a judge and jury. It's my job to simply bring in fugitives so they can have their day in court. As the attorney and town marshal should know."

Jack grinned and nodded. "Point taken."

"Are any of you ready to tell me where he is? For his own sake? If I can take him in peaceably, it would be best for everyone, including him."

Jack said, "Not providing you information is not the same as aiding and abetting."

"That's a fine line, and it would be for a jury to decide."

"That is, *if* we knew where he was."

Crane said, "Just for the record, there's something about the old mountain men that I admire. Your Uncle Joe is the last of them, maybe. The last of the independent men of the frontier, answering to their own sense of justice. I don't usually feel one way or the other toward a fugitive I'm pursuing, but I will admit I hope the jury is merciful to him."

"But you still intend to bring him in," Jack said.

Crane nodded. "It's a matter of pride. I always get my men. No fugitive has ever escaped me for long."

"I would wish you luck," Tom said, "but in this case it would be a conflict of interest."

Crane finished his coffee. He got to his feet and said, "Gentleman, it's been a pleasure."

To Hunter he said, "Thanks for the coffee."

"Don't thank me," Hunter said. "I let you in as a favor to Jack."

Crane stepped out onto the boardwalk. He was still sure Joe McCabe was in the area, and if Joe was, so was the woman. While it was true that a fugitive had never gotten away from him, he thought Joe McCabe would probably be the first, if not for the woman. He doubted anyone could bring in Joe alive, or even find him, if Joe was alone. But having a woman with him would slow him down. Make him vulnerable. She would be his Achilles heel.

One thing Crane was good at was putting himself into the place of those he was chasing. He had now met Johnny McCabe and his son Dusty, and he had talked with his other son Jack and his nephew Tom. Four different personalities, and yet they had certain things in common. Perhaps he could figure out Joe McCabe from them. Put himself in Joe's place.

He lit a cigar and walked across the street, and sat on a bench outside the hotel. The night had been chilly but the morning sun felt warm.

If he were in Joe's place, what would he do? He thought while Jack and Tom left the saloon and walked along the boardwalk. He thought while the man he believed to be Harlan Carter climbed into a buckboard and rode away down Main Street. He thought while the old Chinaman who worked at the Second Chance stepped out front to sweep off the boardwalk.

He looked like a harmless Old man, but he had eyes of steel. You don't get eyes like that unless there was a reason. Crane made a mental note not to underestimate that old man.

He smoked down his cigar, then tossed the butt into the street. And that was when it occurred to him what he would do if he was in Joe's place.

He went to his hotel room and emerged in a range shirt and canvas pants. His gun was buckled on, and he wore a wide-brimmed hat. What the cowboys called a Boss of the Plains hat. He had a bedroll tucked under one arm, saddle bags draped over his shoulder and a Winchester in one hand.

He went to the livery and rented a horse and a saddle.

The old man who worked there had a white beard and a lined face. He said, "You gonna be gone overnight? I see you got your bedroll."

"It depends on what I find on my ride."

Once the horse was saddled, and the bedroll and saddle bags were in place, Crane slid the Winchester into the saddle boot and then stepped up and into the saddle.

Now, he thought, to ride outside of town and begin cutting for sign.

North, he thought. If he were in Joe McCabe's

place, he would be heading north. Most fugitives would head either for the Canadian border and hide there for a time, or they might head to the west coast, Oregon or even California, and try to lose themselves among the population. Maybe take on an assumed name. But Joe McCabe would be heading north and not intending to come back. Joe wouldn't be afraid of the rugged Canadian wilderness.

If Crane didn't intercept Joe and the woman before they got north of the border, he didn't think he would ever catch them.

But he had no intention of letting them get as far as the border.

33

Joe and Kate rested their horses on a wooded ridge. There was an outcropping of bedrock, and from it they had a wide view of the terrain sweeping away behind them. There were wooded hills, one after another, with pine trees standing tall. On one ridge, the trees were scattered, and there was another that was fully forested.

Joe wasn't just gazing, he was doing some serious scouring of their back trail with his eyes.

Kate looked at him curiously, then it dawned on her. "You think we're being followed."

"One thing you gotta do if you're being hunted is put yourself in the mind of the hunter. That's what you do when you're shooting meat for supper. If a deer or an antelope could put itself in our place, we'd never get close enough to shoot one."

She nodded. "Your wisdom and your understanding of the world around you never ceases to amaze me."

"Pa told us boys to never stop learnin'. Look at the world around you and learn all you can from it. Whether you're a lawyer like Jack, or a sailor like Matt used to be. A cattleman like Johnny or a mountain man like me. Never stop learning."

"Your father was a wise man."

Joe nodded, though he didn't take his eyes from the land behind them. "He never stopped learning. The advice he gave us came from his father, and his father before him."

Joe stood for half an hour, watching. Then he said, "If there is someone back there, I cain't see him. But the longer we wait, the less ground we're covering."

They mounted up.

Joe said, "You take the pack team, but don't head north. I've been over this country before. Where this ridge peters out, there'll be a small pass. Cut through it and head west for about two miles. You'll come to a small ravine between ridges. There's a streambed in that ravine. Follow it along until you come to an area where the water pools. If I ain't back yet, then make camp there."

"Where are you going?"

"I'm gonna go do some scouting behind us."

There had been a time when Kate would have been frightened to be out in the wilderness alone, but those days were behind her.

He said, "Be careful. Stay alert. And don't trust anyone. A woman alone out here can't be too careful."

"It's about the same for women everywhere," she said. "You be careful, too."

"I should be catching up with you before nightfall. If I don't, then make camp by that little pond. But don't wait for me too long. If I ain't caught up with you by morning, that means something happened to me."

She hated the sound of that. She said, "Oh, Joe."

"We gotta face the way things are. If something

happens to me, you gotta decide what to do. Think it through. Think through every possibility."

She nodded. "Please be careful."

"Always am."

She clicked her horse ahead, and the pack animals followed. She glanced back over her shoulder at Joe, and he was already gone from sight.

She followed his instructions. She rode down the ridge, making sure not to ride the way they had come up. She carried her rifle across the front of her saddle.

She rode along the base of the ridge, which bent sort of north-northwest. Then she came to the pass Joe had spoken of. It was narrow, with the ridge they had been on and the next one winding their way down toward the pass like two wooded hills.

She took the horses through the pass, moving her eyes from the ground in front of her, looking for tracks, to the distant ridges. Every so often, she would turn to glance behind her.

Once she was through the pass, she saw birds circling in the sky off to the west. Looked like hawks, she thought. She estimated them to be two miles off.

The afternoon wore on as she followed the little stream Joe had spoken of. She glanced back, hoping to see him, but he wasn't there.

The stream was little more than a trickle, but the bed was rocky and much deeper than the stream itself. She figured in the spring the water probably ran deep and fast.

She arrived at the pool, and found it mostly a mud wash, with water at the center only. The pool was a depression in the earth, possibly the result of some sort of sinkhole though she hadn't thought they had them in this part of the country. It was situated beside the stream bed, so in the spring, when the stream was running strong, overflow probably filled the pool.

She let the horses drink from the stream, and then she began stripping off the gear. There was grass near the stream, so she let them graze while she gathered firewood.

She put on hot water for tea, and once she had a cupful, she began brewing some coffee for when Joe arrived.

She opened a can of beans and began heating them in a skillet while she waited.

Once the beans were hot, she sat and ate. It was dark now, so she added some wood to the fire and leaned back against her saddle and her still rolled up soogan.

She began to give thought to something she didn't like. What to do if Joe didn't come back.

The thought would have saddened her beyond her ability to describe, but she had to push those feelings aside for now. She had to survive.

If Joe didn't come back, it meant he found the marshal or the marshal somehow found him, and somehow Joe didn't survive. Which meant the marshal would be coming for her.

She couldn't wait here, she realized. She would

essentially be waiting for the marshal to come to her.

She decided to let the fire burn low, so it wouldn't be as visible from a distance.

She saw movement at the other side of the fire, but she knew what it was.

"Poe," she said.

The wolf moved in beside her and she absently scratched his head while she thought.

She decided if Joe wasn't here by midnight, she would abandon the camp and move on. The only place she could think of was back to the valley. Johnny and Matt would figure out what to do.

She couldn't travel fast with the pack animals, so she would leave them behind. Take her saddle horse only, and a few supplies in her saddle bags.

She wouldn't go back the way she had come, she decided, because she would probably run into the marshal. She would head east for maybe five miles, then turn back south and ride for the valley.

She sat by the fire, her rifle in her lap and Poe at her side.

"Oh, Joe," she said. "Where are you?"

34

Kate heard a sound off to one side. Not quite the snapping of a twig, but maybe a foot stepping down on dry grass and shuffling a bit. Nothing she would have heard by day, but at night the senses seemed somehow enhanced.

She turned her head in that direction, and she saw a man standing maybe thirty feet away. She was amazed that he could have gotten so close to her without the animals reacting. Horses can serve as glorified watch dogs, and she had Poe at her side.

She realized he was situated so the wind was blowing from the horses and the campfire toward him. What Joe called *upwind*. The animals wouldn't catch his scent, and they didn't know he was there until his foot shuffled a bit in the dry grass.

He was maybe as tall as Joe, and the firelight caught a tin badge pinned to his vest. What Kate noticed the most was the revolver in his hand.

She was now enough of a student of firearms that even in the firelight she recognized it as a Colt, probably a .44 or .45. A five-inch barrel. Not the biggest pistol available, but at thirty feet, it could be deadly.

"Don't move an inch," the man said. "Toss away that rifle."

She tossed her Winchester to the ground. She hadn't chambered a round, otherwise the rifle might have fired when it landed on the earth.

He said, "Now that gun in your belt."

Joe's pistol was still tucked into her belt, so she slid it out and tossed it to the ground.

Poe was on his feet, and his ruff was up and he was growling. His teeth were showing and his ears were back.

The man said, "Calm that dog, or I'll shoot it."

Kate said, "Poe, stop."

Poe didn't know voice commands, not that she was sure a wolf could be trained to respond to such a thing.

Poe started advancing toward the man, and he fired his pistol. Poe yelped and spun to one side. Fur went flying, and Poe ran off into the darkness.

Kate dove for the pistol she had tossed away, but the man cocked his gun and fired again, and the bullet kicked up dirt inches from her hand.

"Don't try it," he said. "You're as good to me dead as you are alive."

She climbed back to her feet and said, "You must be that U. S. Marshal."

He nodded. "Hannibal Crane. Now, keep your hands where I can see them. Keep in mind, you have already been found guilty and sentenced to hang. If I have to shoot you, no one will ask any questions."

She raised her hands to the height of her shoulders.

He said, "Where's Joe McCabe?"

"I don't know."

"Don't play games with me."

"I'm not. He left to scout our back trail earlier in the day. I haven't seen him since."

He took a few steps closer, and shot glances to one side and then to the other, and then back to her.

He said, "I know enough of the McCabes to doubt that he just rode off and left you behind."

"I'm not saying he did."

"No," he said, as he walked up to the fire. His gun was in his hand and ready for use, but he had let the muzzle drop a little so it was aimed at the ground. "You're not. The problem is, you're not saying anything. I think what we're going to do is handcuff you, and then wait for him. He's bound to seek you out, sooner or later."

He reached down with his left hand to the coffee kettle, but pulled his fingers back when he found it too hot to touch.

"Tell me," he said, "what is it about you that binds him so to you? A mountain man, half mad or so they say, rides into Cheyenne and with no warning, risks his life and his freedom to save a murderess from the gallows."

"He's not half mad, and I didn't murder anyone."

A shot was fired from somewhere out in the darkness. Kate saw the muzzle flash with her side vision, and the marshal lurched to one side and dropped to his knees. The coffee kettle went spilling onto the ground.

He blinked his eyes, a little startled, and then realized he had left Kate unguarded for a moment. He raised his gun to her, but it was too late. She was on top of him, tackling him, pulling him to the ground.

He was on his back, with her sitting astride him. His left arm no longer seemed to work, but he struck at her with the pistol. He missed, and she clawed at his face.

He managed to raise one knee and push her away. His left arm was still not working, but pushing off the ground with his right hand, he got to his knees. His gun was still in his hand and he raised it to point it at her, but he found a rifle barrel only inches from his face.

Joe McCabe was standing there, holding the rifle.

Joe said, "Give me a reason. We'll leave you here for the wolves and never look back. Might just take your scalp, too. Give me one reason."

Crane let his pistol fall to the ground.

35

Joe's bullet had caught Crane in the shoulder. Crane sat on the ground and Kate had a look at the wound. Joe stood off to one side, his rifle ready to fire.

"Make one wrong move," Joe said, "and my next shot will finish you off."

Crane said, "I suppose it makes no difference to you that I'm wearing the badge of a United States Marshal."

Joe shook his head. "None at all."

Kate pulled the shirt away from the marshal's shoulder. She said, "The bullet is still in there. It has to come out."

Joe said, "We cain't do it here. I ain't no doctor and neither is Kate."

"The nearest doctor," Kate said, "is either in Billings, or back in Jubilee. I'm not sure which place is closest."

"I wouldn't let no city doctor touch me," Joe said. "Haley, back at the ranch, is the only one I'd let take a bullet out of me, now that Granny Tate's gone."

Kate looked at Joe. "We have to get him back to Haley, then."

Joe shook his head. "This man is all about doing his job. He knows nothing about gratitude. We get him back there, it'll delay us getting to the Canadian border. He'll send a wire and have a posse after us."

Crane said, "I will, too. I believe in the law. It's more important than any of us, individually."

"Can you ride?" Joe said.

"I think so."

"All right. We're sending you off on your horse. No guns. Two canteens. If you make it back to the valley, you do."

"Joe," Kate said, "what if he doesn't make it?"

"This man would watch you swing from a rope and not feel a stitch of conscience over it, no matter how kind you might be to him. Because the law is the law, right?"

Crane said, "That is the way it is. The law has to stand above us and our sentimental ways, otherwise there is no civilization. None of us can stand above the law. None of us can decide which laws we want to obey, and which ones we don't."

Joe nodded. "You think about all that on your long ride back to the valley."

In the morning, with a bandana around his arm and tied around his neck as a makeshift sling, and another bandana wrapped about his shoulder to hold back the bleeding, Crane swung up and into the saddle.

"They'll find you," Crane said. "You can't escape the law forever. I heard you say you were going to Canada, and I figured you were, anyway. You have to know I'll be wiring the Canadian authorities as soon as I'm able."

Joe gave a smirk. "Canada's a mighty big place."

"A half-wild mountain man who lives outside the

law, and doesn't believe his lifestyle will ever catch up to him."

"Ain't nothin' *half* about it."

Crane looked at Kate. "You were tried by a jury of your peers and found guilty. Mark my words, you will hang. And you," he looked at Joe, "will probably rot away in a prison."

Kate said, "You'd best be going, Marshal."

He nodded. "Till we meet again."

He clicked the horse ahead. Joe and Kate stood and watched him ride off.

Kate said, "What if he doesn't make it? Will we have that on our consciences?"

Joe shrugged. "I suppose it's all in how you look at it, but I say no. He chose to come after us. He understands the consequences."

"But he might be right. Are we really above the law?"

He shook his head. "My nephew Jack has talked before about the letter of the law versus the intent of the law. Lots of ten-dollar words. He's almost as bad as Matt. But what the gist of it comes down to is I don't think the men who wrote them laws intended an innocent women to get railroaded all the way to a noose. We ain't got the resources to fight that verdict, but we do have the means to escape it."

She nodded. She said, "I suppose we'd best break camp. We got a long ride ahead of us."

They had ridden not a quarter of a mile when they found Poe. He had a deep crease along one shoulder from Crane's bullet. But the bleeding had stopped and the wolf was on his feet.

Joe said, "I should'a knowed it would take more than a lawman's bullet to stop you."

The wolf's legs were a little wobbly.

Kate said, "He's weak. He's lost a lot of blood."

Joe stepped down from his horse and wrapped his arms around Poe and lifted.

"Times like this," Joe said, "I wish you was a chihuahua."

Kate held the reins to Joe's horse while he managed to climb up and into the saddle with the wolf in his arms.

Joe draped the wolf across the front of his saddle. He said, "I thought I had seen everything."

Kate was smiling. "I think it's sweet."

Joe grinned. "I don't know what it is, but Poe's one of us. We couldn't go without him."

"I fully agree."

Joe rode ahead with the wolf on the horse in front of him, and Kate followed leading the string of pack horses.

INTERLUDE

36

Winter passed, and it was spring in Cheyenne. Life was returning to the land. Marshal Kincaid stood in front of his office with a cup of coffee in hand.

Deputy Abbott stood beside him, lighting a cigar.

"I love this time of year," Kincaid said. "Everything's coming alive again."

Abbott nodded. "Last year we saw a lot of excitement here in town. Hopefully this year will be a little calmer."

Kincaid nodded. "Amen to that."

"You ever think about Joe McCabe and that woman? Wonder where they are?"

Kincaid shook his head. "Been a few months since we heard anything about them at all."

"Crane was a fool to go after them by himself. He's lucky that wild man didn't kill him."

Kincaid nodded. It had been more than six months since Crane returned by train from Jubilee, Montana. A doctor had pulled a bullet from Crane's shoulder. The marshal had taken a train from Cheyenne to points east.

"He has a long success record," Kincaid said. "You can't deny him that. But there's something about him that bothers me."

Abbott nodded. "One thing I've been learning by working for you is to trust your gut feelings."

Kincaid had paperwork to do in his office. Reward posters to go through, budget figures to come up with. It was nearing time for him to present his budget to the town. He would ask for more money, they would want to give him less money, and they would both settle right in the middle. Same song and dance every year.

But it was a beautiful spring day and he didn't want to go inside yet.

He said, "Abbott, I'm going to go walk the rounds. Enjoy the morning air."

Abbott nodded. "I'm gonna stay right here and enjoy this here cigar."

Kincaid would walk his rounds with a shotgun in the crook of one arm, on a Saturday night when the cowhands in the area had gotten paid. But this was a Tuesday morning. The town was quiet. Shopkeepers were sweeping off the boardwalks in front of their stores, mainly to find something to do. Kincaid left the shotgun at his office.

The newspaper editor was standing in front of his open doorway, enjoying the morning air. He was a man in his early thirties, with longish hair and a thick mustache.

"Morning, Nathan," Kincaid said.

The man nodded. "Morning, Jubal."

Kincaid strolled more than walked. He still had his coffee cup in one hand, so he stopped at the restaurant and they refilled it for him.

He chatted with a couple of men who were in from a nearby farm for supplies. He tipped his hat to Corinna Simpson, a seamstress who had arrived in town a couple of years earlier.

His rounds eventually brought him to within sight of his office, coming toward it from the opposite end of the street. He saw a horse tied to the hitching post out front.

He found a man was waiting for him in the office. The man had hair that fell to his shoulders from beneath a wide-brimmed hat, and he had a thick mustache that dropped down along either side of his chin. A bandolier was draped about one shoulder and across his chest, and a pistol holstered at his right side. Pinned to his shirt was the badge of a U.S. Marshal.

The man got to his feet. "Marshal Omar Sanborn," he said, extending a hand to Kincaid.

Abbot was at his own desk. He said, "The marshal wanted to meet you, and I told him you would be back in a while."

Kincaid shook the man's hand. "Jubal Kincaid. What brings you to town, Marshal?"

"I've been assigned to this area, and I'm looking into a train robbery that happened off near Laramie."

Kincaid nodded. "Heard about that. Usually it's Marshal Crane who gets assigned to that sort of thing. He knows the area."

Sanborn nodded. "Crane turned in his badge a couple of months ago. I'm taking his place."

They chatted a bit while Abbott made some fresh coffee. The chatting took place on the bench outside the office, because the stove heated up the office too much.

Once the coffee was done, Sanborn was on his way. Kincaid stood in the doorway, watching him ride off.

Abbott said, "You're getting one of them feelings again, aren't you?"

Kincaid nodded.

Abbott said, "You think there's something wrong with Sanborn?"

"Oh, no. Not at all. It's something else."

"Mind telling me what?"

"Could be nothing." He looked at Abbott. "Do you think you could handle things for two or three days? I have a small trip I have to take."

Abbott blinked with surprise. "Yeah, I suppose so. It's been slow around here."

Kincaid slapped Abbott's shoulder and said, "I'll be down at the train station."

He knew the afternoon train would arrive around three o'clock, for points north.

He went to the ticket window, and said to the man behind the desk, "I need a ticket to Jubilee, Montana."

37

Jack McCabe was sitting at his desk. The clock on the wall had just bonged five times, meaning it was nearing dinner time. He had a will to draw up, but figured he could do that in the morning. He didn't want to keep Nina waiting. Partly out of respect for the woman he loved, and partly because her cooking was so good.

The door opened, and Jack saw a man he hadn't seen in years. The man was in a string tie and jacket, and had put on a few pounds since Jack had last seen him, and the man's mustache was now showing some silver. But Jack would know him anywhere.

"Marshal Kincaid," Jack said.

Kincaid and Jack shook hands.

Jack said, "What brings you to Jubilee?"

"I'd like to say it's a social call, but I think there's trouble brewing. And I figured you and your family were the people to turn to."

Kincaid took a chair in front of Jack's desk. Jack poured them each a bourbon, and Kincaid told Jack what was on his mind.

Nina's dinner would have to wait, Jack realized. He sent word to her that he would be home very late, and then he and Kincaid went to the livery to rent a couple of horses.

It was dark when Jack and Kincaid sat in the small parlor of the cabin in the canyon north of the valley. A fire was crackling away in the stone hearth, and Johnny sat in the chair he had made himself, and he had a cup of coffee in one hand.

Eli was standing by the mantel. He now stood as tall as Johnny. He was in a range shirt and a vest, and his pistol was buckled on. So was Johnny's.

Kincaid said, "I found out earlier today that Marshal Crane has turned in his badge."

Johnny nodded. "Probably for the best."

"Something about the man," Kincaid said. "My gut feeling is that something is really wrong."

Johnny nodded again. "My father taught us to always trust your gut."

Kincaid said, "I have to ask this. Not as a lawman. I don't have any jurisdiction out here, anyway. I'm just asking as a friend. Where is your brother Joe and Miss Kate?"

Jessica was in a rocker beside Johnny. He looked at her and she nodded her head.

He said to Kincaid, "They lit out for the Bow River area in Canada, early last August. I figure they're in those mountains, now. Knowing Joe, he probably got a cabin up and had them ready for winter before the first snow."

"Bow River," Kincaid said. "Don't know much about it."

"Very remote area. Over the past couple of years,

from what I've heard, a couple of towns have sprouted up. But if a man wanted to lose himself, I can't think of a deeper stretch of mountains."

"Have you heard from him?"

Johnny shook his head. "Don't really expect to, either."

"Then, how can you be sure he and Miss Kate got to those mountains?"

Jessica smiled. "You don't know Joe."

Kincaid returned the smile. "I met him last summer, and I have to say, he's probably the most capable man I ever met."

Eli said, "I don't think there's anything my Uncle Joe couldn't do, if he set his mind to it."

Kincaid had a cup of coffee in one hand, and he took a sip. "I was present last year for Miss Kate's entire trial. It was my deputy and I who first arrested her. I didn't believe for a second it was she who killed her husband."

"Why?" Johnny said. Not that he believed Kate was guilty, but he wanted to hear Kindaid's reasoning.

"For one thing, the evidence was too neatly arranged. I haven't seen a lot of murder scenes. Most of the shootings in Cheyenne are on a Saturday night when cowhands get a little too rowdy. But I've seen some, and they're messy. Clues aren't just there in plain sight. A kitchen knife covered in blood was found in her bedroom, right where we could find it. That's just a little too convenient for me."

Kincaid looked at Jack. "What would you do in her place?"

"Either dispose of that knife, or wash the blood off."

Kincaid nodded. "Doesn't take a genius to figure that out. And she had dozed off in her room. After you kill a man, you don't just leave the murder weapon with blood on it, and go doze off somewhere."

Kincaid looked at Johnny. "When you've killed a man, you have a certain look in the eye. A look you can try to cover up, but it's there. We lawmen, we usually know if a suspect is guilty or not. We know it in our gut, by looking them in the eye. We're not always right, but we usually are. The clues might say something different, and a good lawyer can twist things all around in court to make a jury believe what he wants them to believe."

He looked at Jack. "No offense."

Jack said, "None taken."

Johnny said, "My nephew Tom is the marshal in Jubilee. He's said the same sort of thing."

Kincaid looked from Johnny to Jessica, "I'd stake my reputation that she never killed that man."

"Okay," Johnny said. "We're all in agreement. But what's that have to do with Crane?"

Kincaid shrugged. "I guess maybe it just explains my interest in this case. My belief that she's innocent, and my respect for your brother Joe. And my gut feeling that Crane somehow has a piece missing from his puzzle."

He waited a moment, then said, "I think Crane is

going after your brother and Miss Kate."

"It'll be his funeral," Eli said.

"If your uncle knows he's coming. Which he doesn't. And your uncle will be expecting Crane to be coming in as a lawman, not as some sort of glorified bounty hunter. He turned his badge in a couple of months ago."

Johnny took a sip of coffee while he let this bounce around in his head a little.

He said, "I talked with Crane a couple of times last summer. He seemed to take a lot of pride in the fact that no fugitive had ever escaped from him."

Kincaid said, "Until now."

"You think he's going after them out of some sort of misshapen sense of pride."

Kincaid nodded. "That's just what I think."

Johnny looked at Jessica. She said nothing, but he could tell by the look in her eye that she knew what was coming.

Johnny looked at Eli and said, "Are you up to riding out to your Uncle Matt's cabin and fetching him?"

Eli shrugged. "I sure am."

"In the morning, Your uncle Matt and I are heading out to the Bow River country."

PART FOUR

Bow River

38

June 1885

Joe stood on a ledge, looking off at a green slope that pulled away from him down below. In the distance was another mountain, covered with pine and rounded toward the summit.

He had been in these mountains before, years earlier, when he and Dusty and Matt had sprung Sam Middleton from a prison in Mexico, and brought him north of the border to hide out from the law.

In the valley down below, the Bow River meandered its way through. The last time Joe had been to these mountains, they had been populated only by a few wandering Indians. Now there were two towns on the river. Or *on the Bow*, as the locals said. They weren't really towns by the standards of civilized folk. More rough-edged frontier communities, kind of like McCabe Gap had been before it had sprung into the boom town of Jubilee.

One town was called Cochrane, and the other was Bow River. There was a third community, hardly more than a trading post and a few teepees, that folks were starting to call Mitford.

There was no ranching in the valley, but some lumber operations had started up, and there was some mining.

Joe had been down to the valley a couple of times, having a look around. Since he and Kate were on the run, he wanted to know what to expect from the people of the valley.

The towns were small and he expected no problems from the people who were there now. But the railroad had come to the valley. It had reached Cochran and had stretched past Bow River, and would soon be touching Mitford. With the railroad would come more people. The towns would grow. He wondered how long he and Kate would be safe in these mountains.

Joe looked down at the slope below, and off at the mountain that was a little hazy in the distance.

It was early morning. The sun was barely in the sky, and the sky was a deep blue. Even though it was nigh onto summer, and he was sure the day would be warm down on the Bow, the mountain wind was cool and crisp. Just the way he liked it.

Behind him was a stand of pines, and beyond them was the cabin he had put up for the winter. They had arrived in these mountains toward the end of the previous summer. Cold weather hit early at this altitude, and Joe had to work hard and fast to get the cabin built. But he had managed to make it sturdy.

It was small—simply one room with a bunk at one wall for him and Kate, and a stone hearth at the other. In the center of the room was a table and two chairs Joe had fashioned from pinewood.

Kate came walking through the pines and he wrapped one arm around her shoulders. She was in a Cheyenne-style buckskin dress with tall boots that reached to her knees. Her hair was a foot longer than it had been when he had broken her out of jail, and it was tied in two braids that fell along her back.

He said, "I'm thinking of adding onto the cabin. Maybe a bedroom and a parlor. Sort of like Johnny's cabin at the canyon, but with only one bedroom."

She shook her head. "I like it just the way it is. I can't imagine we'll be receiving any guests up here. We won't need any more room."

"You never know. Children could come along."

She gave him a smile. "It's a nice thought, but I think I'm probably too old for that."

"You ain't old. You never will be, in my eyes."

She pulled him in for a hug.

Joe said, "I think I might make us a front porch, though. And a rocker for you, and a chair like Johnny has, for me."

"I wouldn't mind that."

They had cleared off a couple of acres on a flat area within sight of the cabin and were attempting a crop of potatoes and corn. Nothing they would make any money from, just enough to feed themselves. It was hard to keep the critters out of the garden, though, and Joe thought it might prove to be a losing effort.

They discussed it that night, after a meal of venison and wild onions and greens. Joe was sitting on a stump outside the cabin with his long Cheyenne pipe in one hand. He had hauled one of the chairs out from the cabin for Kate. Nights like this made him think even more that he wanted to build a front porch.

Joe said, "In the morning, I'll be riding down to Bow River."

He had done some trapping and hunting over the winter, and had enough beaver pelts and deer hides to load up two packhorses. He was going see about trading them for supplies.

"I would so like to make the garden successful," Kate said. "I hate the idea of you riding down to one of those towns for supplies. I'm afraid someone is going to recognize you."

"Has to be done. Even if we can make a go of it with the garden, there are things we're gonna need, like coffee and tea. Cloth. Gunpowder."

She nodded. "Please be careful down there."

"Always am."

They had talked about her riding with him, but he thought it would be safer if she remained at the camp. The two of them might draw more attention to anyone who might have read any reward posters for them. And Joe had no doubt reward posters had reached this far north.

Poe came out of the woods and walked over to Joe. The crease that had been cut through his fur along one shoulder by Crane's bullet had healed. It left a streak of thin, white fur. If not for the crease, Joe wouldn't know the wolf had been hurt at all.

Joe scratched Poe between the ears, and Poe wagged his tail.

Kate said, "I wonder if we'll always have to be on the run. I wonder if we'll ever truly be safe?"

39

As the morning sun was peeking over the horizon, Joe was already a couple of miles from their camp. He rode with his scattergun across the saddle bows in front of him, and he led two pack animals loaded down with pelts and buckskins. In his saddle boot was a Winchester, and his long knife was sheathed at his side.

The ridge dropped off steep toward the bottom, so he rode along parallel to the land below for a while, then he found a less severe grade and worked his way down to the valley floor.

He tried to never take the same route in or out of their camp. Just in case.

This valley was different than the one Johnny had named Shoshone Valley. Where Johnny's valley was surrounded by softly rounded ridges and hills, and the center was mostly grassy, this valley was lined by tall mountains, a couple of which still showed white even though it was late spring. The valley floor was covered with a dense pine forest, and the Bow River wound its way through it.

Joe came to a trail and followed it into the town of Bow River. The town had a wide main street that was lined with buildings, some made of logs and others with planks slapped together. Some had windows that were not evenly placed. One, a saloon, looked to be leaning a little to one side. A line of railroad tracks swung near a long building toward the end of the street, the building serving as the railroad depot.

A series of smaller trails swung out from the main street, and along those trails were scattered buildings, mostly houses or cabins.

There were three saloons in town, and a brothel. One of the saloons served as a church on Sunday, and as a local courthouse.

Bow River was much like the wilder towns of the American frontier, and yet they were not so wild. Canada had sent the North-West Mounted Police to the frontier in 1874, essentially establishing law-enforcement before the settlers arrived.

It was noon as Joe rode along Bow River's Main Street. He had a few coins in the pocket of his buckskin shirt. Enough for two bottles of beer. He figured he would stop at one of the saloons, if he could find one open this early.

The first one he came to was built of logs and had a peaked roof. A hand-painted sign above the door read MULE SKINNER SALOON.

The door was open, so Joe tethered his horses at a hitching rail out front and stepped in. He held his scattergun in the crook of one arm.

The bartender was a tall man with a long, dark beard.

Joe said, "You open?"

The man nodded. "Come on in."

There were a couple of men leaning against the bar. Looked like lumberjacks. Plaid, flannel shirts and narrow-brimmed hats. Leather work boots that laced up the front.

They were talking and laughing, and one of them had a distinctive Scottish-sounding brogue. Joe had found you heard that type of talk a lot up here, north of the border.

"What can I get you?" The bartender said.

"A bottle of beer. Whatever brand you have."

"Got me some Molson. Five cents. I've gotta see the money first, though. No offense."

"None taken." Joe set two nickels on the bar. "I'm gonna be wantin' a second one."

The bartender nodded with a grin, pulled the cork from a bottle of beer and set it on the bar in front of Joe.

Joe took a few sips, allowing himself to enjoy the taste.

He heard horses out front, and men talking. Then four men came into the saloon, their spurs jingling. They wore riding boots, with dusty pants tucked into them. Two had bandoliers across the chest. They all had pistols at their belts, one of them wearing his turned for a cross-draw.

They had scraggly whiskers and trail dust on their hats. They had been riding a while, Joe figured.

They bellied-up to the bar and asked for scotch.

The bartender said, "Gotta see some cash, first."

One of them, with a thick black mustache and dark eyes, drew his gun and aimed it directly at the bartender's nose. He said, "No you don't."

Joe was about to step in, when a man said from the doorway, "Put that gun away."

Joe glanced over. The man was about the age of Josh and Dusty. Chin neatly shaven, and he wore a brown, wide-brimmed hat and a gun at his side.

The way he stood there, Joe figured he was a lawman. Then Joe noticed a badge pinned to the man's gunbelt. It wasn't a tin star or a shield, like most lawmen in the States. It was a fancy thing, with what looked like laurel leaves winding about the outer edges. Must be a Mountie, he figured.

The man with the gun stepped away from the bartender, though he kept his gun in his hand.

"Ah, the famed North-West Mounted Police," the man said. Joe noticed a French lilt to the man's speech. "The problem is there is only one of you, and four of us. How fast you think you can shoot with your pistol, eh, Mountie?"

The two lumberjacks scrambled to the far side of the barroom. The bartender ran from behind the bar to join them.

The Mountie stepped fully into the barroom. "Jacques Pierre, I presume."

The man grinned and affected a little bow. "At your service."

"Wanted for a stage robbery outside of Calgary."

The man was smiling, but not with amusement. It was more of a taunting smile.

He said, "Why, that would be us. But again, I must point out, there are four of us. Only one of you."

Joe stepped away from the bar, his scattergun now in both hands, and he cocked both hammers. "He ain't alone."

"Now, who is this?" the man said.

"A man who ain't gonna stand by and watch a lawman get gunned down."

The Mountie said, "Throw down your guns."

The man with the gun instead raised his for a shot, but Joe fired. A load of buckshot caught the man in the chest, and he was pushed backward and landed on a table. The table flipped over, the man with it.

The others were pulling their guns, but the Mountie fired. He fanned two shots—the only other man Joe had seen do that with any degree of accuracy was Dusty—and each bullet caught a man in the chest.

The third man had his gun drawn and out to full extension, and Joe let loose with his second barrel. The man seemed to explode in a spray of blood and was knocked backward to the floor.

None of the men were getting up. Joe didn't think they would be.

The Mountie said to Joe, "That's quite a weapon you have, there."

Joe nodded. "Never knew anyone who could argue much with ten gauge double-ought."

"Me neither. I'm Corporal Brian Easton, of the North-West Mounted Police."

Joe nodded. He decided to use the name he and his brothers had used in Texas, years ago, when there had been a price on their heads.

He said, "Joe O'Brien."

The bodies were hauled off, the Mountie left and Joe went back to work on his beer. His scattergun was one of the newer ones that was a breech-loader, so he opened it, pulled out the empties and dropped in two fresh shells.

He had intended to come into town and not draw any attention to himself. Didn't go very well.

Once his beer was finished, he decided against the second beer after all and took back one of the nickels. He wanted to get out of town as soon as possible.

He headed down to the general store to trade his furs, not taking the time to dicker but instead taking the price offered, and filled the packs with flour, coffee, some cans of tea and a couple of boxes of ammunition. He also took two canvas tarps and two bolts of fabric.

He swung into the saddle and was riding along the main street when the Mountie stepped off the boardwalk toward him.

"Mister O'Brien," he said. "Might I have a word with you?"

Joe reined up.

The Mountie had two sheets of paper in his hands. About the size of reward posters.

He said, "I wanted to thank you again for helping me out, back there."

Joe nodded. "Weren't nothin'. I ain't gonna sit back and watch a lawman get gunned down by the likes of them jaspers."

"Are you staying in the area?"

Joe decided to speak carefully. "Got me a small camp up in the mountains. I'm doing some trapping."

Corporal Easton nodded. "I consider myself a good judge of character, Mister O'Brien. I understand fully well that there are often mitigating circumstances to a situation."

Mitigating. This here Mountie liked to throw around ten-dollar words like Matt did.

The Mountie said, "Things are often not as they appear on the surface."

Joe had to agree. "Ain't that the truth."

"I pride myself in being a judge of character, and we Mounties have been given a wide berth when enforcing the law out here on the frontier."

The Mountie folded the two sheets of paper together and handed them up to Joe.

Easton said, "Some interesting reading for you. Take care, Mister O'Brien."

Joe nodded, and he clicked his horse ahead, the pack animals falling into place behind him.

Once the final building in Bow River was behind him, he opened the papers for a look.

They were reward posters, one for him and one for Kate.

Joe folded the papers back up and stuffed them into a pocket in his buckskin shirt, and he rode on.

40

Crane stepped out of the train station and let his gaze wander up one side of the street and then the other. The small town of Bow River, not nearly as large as Jubilee or Cheyenne.

Where he had always traveled in a tie and jacket before, he now was in a range shirt and a tattered vest. He wore canvas pants for riding, and tall boots with spurs. He had a revolver holstered at his belt and a Winchester in one hand, and saddle bags draped over one shoulder.

Missing from the front of his shirt was the U.S. Marshal's badge that had been there for the previous ten years. Funny how heavy that badge seemed, he thought, considering it was really just a little piece of tin. It felt so conspicuously absent. He also thought about how emotionally heavy it had seemed. How it had tied him down. Now he was free to act without considering the badge and what it meant.

He realized he was being watched. People were moving about the boardwalk in front of the train station, pushing past him. But across the dirt street, one man was standing and looking at him. The man looked young, about the age of the McCabe boy who had been with Johnny in Jubilee. He wore a brown wide-brimmed brown hat, a tan shirt, and he had a gun at his side. His gun was at his left side and turned backward for a crossdraw, and it had a leather flap over the top. Looked military, he thought.

Must be the local Mountie, Crane figured. He had done a little research on this town before he boarded the train. The Mountie's name was Corporal Brian Easton. Born in Canada. Raised on a cattle ranch maybe two hundred miles east of here. Assigned to this town out of Fort Macleod. He most often had a couple of Mounties with him in town.

Crane was usually good at assessing men, often at a glance. In his line of work, he needed to be. The fact that Easton was out of uniform could mean his mentality was more cowboy than military. But the way he wore his gun told Crane that the man had at least a little sense of military decorum.

Crane had hoped that he could go about his business without attracting the attention of local law enforcement. Looked like that wasn't going to happen.

The Mountie crossed the street and said to Crane, "Good morning."

Crane nodded. "Good morning, Corporal."

"Might I ask your business in town?"

"You might. But I'm not obliged to answer."

Easton looked at him. Young, but not in any way intimidated. "It's the job of the North-West Mounted Police to keep the peace. For one thing, we have banned the wearing of firearms. If you stay in town, you have to leave those guns in your room. If you keep on wearing the guns, you'll either have to leave town or wind up in our jail."

"My name is Hannibal Crane, and I'm a U.S. Marshal. I'm here to apprehend a couple of fugitives."

"Funny, I don't see a badge."

Crane gave a pained sigh. He had fallen into old habits. He said, "I'm a *former* U.S. Marshal, actually. I'm here to bring in two fugitives. One is a woman who was found guilty of murder in the Territory of Wyoming. The other is half-wild mountain man who broke her out of jail."

"Do these fugitives have names?"

Crane nodded. "The woman is Katrina Compton, and the man's name is Joe McCabe."

"McCabe, huh?"

"You've heard the name. I see the legend has made its way this far north."

"So, why would a man give up his badge and still trail outlaws? The bounty on their heads?"

Crane nodded. "For one thing, yes. I don't have a salary anymore. The other is pride. You see, like you Mounties, I always get my man. For you, it's probably reputation more than fact. But for me, it was fully a fact. Until McCabe and the Compton woman escaped from me. McCabe put a bullet in me last summer and almost killed me. Now I'm here to bring them back."

"Where do you think they might be?"

"Probably in the mountains surrounding this valley. Like I said, he's a mountain man."

The Mountie said, "I don't like bounty hunters,

Mister Crane. I consider them little more than vigilantes. And unlike the constables and town marshals of your country, my jurisdiction doesn't end at the town line. Take my advice and get on the next train back to the States."

"I think I might stay a while, and partake of the hospitality in your fine little town."

"Stay out of trouble, Crane. And lose those guns."

The Mountie gave him a last, long look, and then moved on.

Crane thought Corporal Easton seemed to have taken an instant dislike to him. He chuckled at the thought. Most people seemed to dislike him, but he didn't mind. His job wasn't to make people like him, it was to hunt down fugitives.

Maybe he was self-employed now, but he figured he was still doing his job. Except now, instead of a monthly salary, he got paid for each fugitive. And the pay would be a whole lot better.

Corporal Easton went back to his office and found Private Wilson at a desk. Wilson was young, on his first assignment west. Blonde hair cut short, and he was in the red tunic of the Mounties.

There was usually a third Mountie assigned to the town, too, under Easton's command. The one who had been here recently had been reassigned, and they were waiting for his replacement. Not a good time for Easton to be out of town, but that couldn't be helped.

Easton said, "Al, I have some business to take care of. I might be gone for a couple of days. Do you think you can handle things?"

Wilson shrugged. "I suppose so. It's Tuesday. The town's about as quiet as it can be this time of week."

Easton nodded. During the week, Bow River could be so quiet that two Mounties seemed like one too many. But on a Friday or Saturday night when the miners, the lumber jacks and the railroad workers got paid, the town could light up and it was almost too much for three Mounties to handle.

"I should be back before Friday," Easton said.

He grabbed his bedroll and saddle bags, and a Winchester from the gun rack. With the bedroll under one arm and the saddle bags draped over his shoulder, and the rifle in one hand, he headed for the livery.

41

Joe stood outside the cabin with his Cheyenne pipe in one hand. It was early morning, and he was planning to use the day for cutting firewood.

The morning breeze was cool, and the smell of wood smoke was in the air. Thin, white smoke was drifting from the stone chimney of the cabin.

Poe was sitting beside Joe, glancing about in the bored way a dog will when he's looking for something to do.

So much like the dog we grew up with, Joe thought. Old Jeb. A mongrel—part German Shepherd and part something else. Joe never knew what. The last time Joe had seen that dog was when he and his brothers were back in Pennsylvania, back when their pa was shot. Close to thirty years ago. Joe marveled at how much time had passed. Didn't seem like it could be thirty years.

Poe looked up at some point in the woods off to the right. His ears were perked, and he didn't look happy. Joe's scattergun was leaning against the side of the cabin, so he set his pipe down on the ground and grabbed the gun.

Poe was now growling.

"What is it, boy?" Joe said. As if the wolf could answer him.

Joe could hear motion, now. He knew it to be a rider. A horse moves differently when it has a rider. Joe heard the crack of a stick, and the sound a hoof makes when it rustles on some dried leaves. Then another stick breaking, and then the tell-tale sign. A nicker.

The rider came into view. It was the Mountie from town. Corporal Easton.

Joe said, "Easy, Poe."

Poe didn't always listen, so Joe reached a hand down to the back of the wolf's neck and again said, "Easy."

Then Joe stepped in front of Poe.

Easton said, "You have a pet wolf?"

Joe shook his head. "Not a pet. Just a friend."

Easton reigned up. He kept his eyes on Poe, but he didn't make any move for the gun in his holster.

"Odd time of day to be out for a ride," Joe said.

"You're not the easiest man to find."

"Kind of planned it that way."

Joe didn't realize Kate had left the cabin until she stepped around from the corner with a Winchester aimed at the Mountie.

She said, "I have you covered, Joe."

"He's a friend," Joe said to her. Then to Easton he said, "You *are* a friend, aren't you? Because otherwise you done brung a heap load of trouble onto yourself."

Easton grinned. "Yes, I'm a friend. I'd be a fool to come up here otherwise."

"Well, then, we got coffee on the fire inside."

Kate lowered her rifle.

Easton looked down at the wolf. The animal's teeth were no longer bared, but he was looking at Easton like he was going to take no nonsense.

Easton said, "What will it take to convince him that I'm a friend?"

"Don't know," Joe said. "He's a lot harder to convince than we are."

42

Easton climbed out of the saddle, his eyes on the wolf.

Joe said, "Now, kneel down. And don't show any fear."

Easton said, "I've never been this close to a wolf before."

"He can smell fear, Corporal," Kate said, walking around from the side of the cabin.

"That's good to know."

Joe said, "Stay calm, and kneel down."

Easton knelt down.

Joe said, "Now say, *here, doggy, doggy.*"

Easton gave him a look. "Do I really have to say that?"

Joe was grinning. "No. I just wanted to give it a try."

Kate laughed.

Joe said, "Just hold out your hand and wait for him."

Easton held out his hand. Poe looked at him with caution for a few moments, then started walking toward him.

Poe then sniffed Easton's hand.

Joe said, "If you had something to feed him, it would help."

Kate said, "Hold on a moment."

She went into the cabin and came out with a biscuit. "I made these fresh this morning. Poe loves them."

She tossed one to Easton and said, "Hold that out to him."

Easton did, and Poe took it from his fingers with one bite.

Easton said, "His teeth touched my fingers."

Joe nodded. "Could've taken your fingers off, if he wanted to."

"I'm glad you didn't decide to take a grizzly for a pet."

"Fought one once. They don't make good pets."

Once they were inside, Kate poured him a cup of coffee. The table was small and there were two chairs only.

Kate said, "We didn't expect guests out here."

"Which brings to mind," Joe said, "how *did* you find us?"

"I've been riding through the mountains for the past two days, cutting for sign. Looking for any indication of human life out here. At one point I caught a horse trail that looked to be a couple of days old, but then I lost the trail in a stream."

Joe nodded. "Best way to cover your tracks. Them tracks you was following would be mine."

"I figured. Then this morning, I saw the smoke from your chimney." Easton took a sip of the coffee. "This is very good, ma'am. Thank you."

Kate had taken the other chair. She said, "You're more than welcome."

Joe was standing, leaning one hand against a rough-hewn timber he had put into place as a fireplace mantel.

He said, "Now, about a second question I have for you."

"Why am I looking for you."

Joe nodded. "That'd be it."

"Are either of you familiar with a U.S. Marshal by the name of Hannibal Crane?"

A look of dread crossed Kate's face. "Oh yes. All too well."

"He arrived in town two days ago, and he's looking for you both."

Joe rolled his eyes with weariness. "I knowed I should've killed him when I had the chance."

Easton told them that Crane had apparently resigned from the marshal's service and was now acting on his own.

"Bounty hunting," Joe said.

Easton nodded. "So it seems."

Joe said to Easton, "And by riding up here, and leaving a trail with your horse, you've practically led him right to us."

Easton shook his head. "Not a chance. I took a roundabout way. I did the same trick you do, riding through streams. I saw your chimney smoke yesterday around noon. I made sure I didn't leave a direct trail up here."

Joe nodded. "I hope so. That man might look citified, but he's a good tracker."

Kate was genuinely afraid. "What are we going to do?"

"First off, we're going to put out the fire in the fire place. We're going to have to go without a fire for a few days."

"When I leave here," Easton said, "I'll ride east along the ridge for a few miles, then come down out of the mountains outside of town."

"There's only one way to deal with a man like that," Joe said. "I'm gonna have to shoot him."

Easton held up a hand in a stopping motion. "Hold on. You're not in the States anymore. We Mounties have jurisdiction throughout the land. We're not limited by county lines or territorial boundaries. Give me a chance to find him."

"But how can you arrest him?" Kate said. "What crime has he committed?"

"I can't arrest him until I can prove he's done something wrong. But if I can find him and insist on riding with him, he might just turn back to town. Bounty hunting is illegal here in Canada, and he won't be able to conduct a search for you with me tagging along."

When Easton's coffee was finished, he went outside to mount up. Poe was gone.

"Where's your wolf?" Easton said.

Joe shrugged. "He comes and goes."

"I'll handle Crane," Easton said again to Joe. "Trust me."

Joe nodded. "I'll trust you. To a point. But if he finds us, then all bets are off."

Kate said, "Why, Corporal? Why are you not arresting us yourself?"

He shrugged. "Call it discretion. Trying to maintain the law out here requires a lot of it, sometimes. And I owe Joe."

Easton turned his horse toward the woods, then looked back over his shoulder at them. "Besides, from what I hear of the McCabes, it might be a good thing to have one handy if I ever need someone to get my back."

Easton rode into the woods, and then wound his horse around so he was heading east.

The ridgeline was covered with a pine forest, thick enough that he wouldn't be observed from the valley floor, but not so thick that he couldn't ride his horse through the trees.

Off to the right and above him was Waputik Peak, its summit looking jagged. It was still white with snow.

He turned his horse down the slope, figuring he had gone far enough. He would emerge onto the valley floor in the thick pine forest that covered it. He would then bear southeast, and would circle around the town of Bow River and come in from the opposite side, near the train station.

He stopped after a few miles. Might be a good place to rest the horse a bit, he thought. Loosen the cinch. The ridge was starting to flatten out as he neared the valley floor, and there was a small grassy area, almost a meadow, surrounded by the thick pine forest.

A gunshot exploded from the edge of the woods, the bullet catching Easton hard in the chest, and he was knocked out of the saddle. His horse reared in panic and ran off across the meadow.

Crane came riding out of the trees, keeping his horse to a walk. He had a Winchester in his hands, and he jacked in another round.

"Make a move, Corporal, and I'll put another bullet in you."

Crane nudged his horse toward the corporal.

Crane said, "I heard in town about how the mountain man with the long hair and the long beard helped you out in a gun battle. I figured you might have gone off to warn him. You Canadians were always a little soft."

Crane grinned. "Call it providence, Corporal. Or just plain old-fashioned bad luck on your part. I was here letting my horse graze when I heard a rider coming. Sure makes my job easier."

Crane reined up, and saw Easton was lying face down in the grass and not moving.

"Well," Crane said. "Maybe my first shot was good enough. I don't have to waste another bullet finishing you off."

Crane turned his horse into the trees, following the corporal's trail back up toward the ridge.

43

Johnny would have liked to have brought along a couple of horses from the remuda. Thunder was getting old and so Johnny didn't bring him on long trips, but there were other good horses. However it cost more to bring horses by train, and a ticket bought on short-notice was always expensive. So Johnny and Matt rented two from the livery in Bow River.

"This place is incredible," Johnny said, as they rode along the side of the river. "Just like you and Joe and Dusty described it. But the telling isn't the same as seeing it."

Matt nodded his head. "When we were here, there weren't any towns. No railroad. Joe used to talk about what it would be like to live here long-term. We scouted out places that might be good for building a cabin."

"That's how we're going to find him, by riding out to those places," Johnny said. "Lead on."

Matt's face was lined and his mustache was white. He had a leaner frame than Johnny and much leaner than Joe. He rode in the relaxed, easy way he always did. A wide-brimmed hat was pulled down over his temples, and he was in a range shirt and a leather vest.

Johnny had given Matt a nickel-plated Colt revolver for Christmas, and it was holstered at Matt's right side.

Johnny had his Sharps rifle in the saddle boot. He

had gotten some stares from train passengers, traveling with his rifle, but he had a feeling he might need it.

Johnny scanned the trees around them for a sign of anything that might be out of place. Then he would drop is gaze to the ground ahead of them, looking for tracks. Maybe he wasn't as jumpy as he had been years ago, but now was a time for wariness.

He noticed a bird off to one side, circling about. Then he saw a second. Buzzards.

"There's something over there," Johnny said.

Matt nodded. "I see them."

They rode through the trees and came to a small grassy patch.

A man was sitting in the grass. Blood was soaking into the left side of his shirt. With his right hand, he was holding a bandana over the wound to slow down the bleeding.

Johnny swung out of the saddle.

The man said, "Let me guess. Johnny McCabe."

Johnny was a little surprised.

The man said, "I know your brother. And if the legends about your family are true, when one of you is in trouble the others aren't going to be far behind."

The man introduced himself as Corporal Easton.

Matt said, "Was it Crane?"

Easton nodded. "He ambushed me. I'd be dead now, if not for this."

He reached down to the grass beside him and held

up a small book. It looked like a spike had been driven through it.

"A Bible," he said. "My mother gave it to me, years ago. She said the word of the Lord would save my life. Turned out it does, in more ways than one. This took the brunt of the bullet."

Johnny said, "Can you ride?"

Easton nodded. "Your brother's camp is up the ridge, maybe ten miles back. The bullet knocked the wind out of me and I was out for a few minutes. I woke up as Crane was riding away. It's been maybe an hour. You follow my horse's back trail and you'll come to the camp."

Johnny said to Matt, "Can you get him back to town? I'll go after Crane myself."

"If you get yourself killed," Matt said, "Jessica will never speak to me."

Johnny grinned.

44

Joe sat at the table. He had poured the remainder of the morning's coffee into his cup, and Kate was having a cup of tea. He had scattered the remaining wood in the stove, and the fire had burned down so there was no more smoke.

"I'm thinking I should go look for Crane," Joe said. "I hate the thought of just sitting here, waiting for him to come to us."

"Don't you trust the corporal?"

Joe nodded. "Yeah, I do. Something about him, I think he's a man to ride the river with. He's got some education, like Jack. You can hear it in the way he talks. But, like Jack, he's got a backbone. It's just that I ain't used to letting another man fight my battles for me. I had to sit by while Johnny and the others got supplies for us in Jubilee last summer. And now I'm having to sit by again."

"I can understand that." She took a sip of tea. "A man of the mountains has to be self-sufficient. But I think it's for the best to let the corporal handle things."

He gave a reluctant, "I suppose so."

She smiled. "I'm going to go down to the stream for some water, so I can wash the morning dishes."

She grabbed an empty bucket.

He said, "You want me to fetch that for you? A bucket of water can be heavy."

She shook her head. "A woman of the mountains

has to be self-sufficient, too."

She threw him a smile and stepped out the door.

He took another sip of coffee, and he glanced at the timbers overhead and the log walls. He liked this little cabin. But the reality was they wouldn't be able to stay long. Corporal Easton was a good man, but the way the Mounties worked, he could be reassigned at any time, and his replacement might be more of a by-the-book lawman.

Joe had heard talk of Alaska in recent years. There might be gold up there. Maybe that was where he and Kate should head. But Joe knew nothing of the land up there. The woods, the mountains.

Joe heard Kate call out. "Joe? Can you come out here?"

Joe got to his feet. He snatched his scattergun that he had left leaning against one wall and stepped outside.

Crane was there, about twenty feet from the cabin door. He was holding Kate with one arm wrapped around her neck, and a pistol aimed at her temple.

"Drop the shotgun, wild man," Crane said, "or I'll put a bullet right in her head."

Dang, Joe thought. *Must be getting careless in my old age.*

"I mean it," Crane said. "I hate not to be a gentleman, but there's too much money on your heads."

"I've seen the reward posters," Joe said. $5,000 for him, and $10,000 for Kate. A whole pile of money. More than a cowhand would make in ten years. He noticed that, oddly, all of the money was being put up by Compton Enterprises. Apparently Eli's brother really wanted her hanged.

Crane said, "It would be easier for me to bring you both in dead, so give me a reason to shoot her."

Joe set his scattergun down on the ground.

"Now," he said to Kate, "I'm going to let you go, and you're going to tie his hands behind his back. If either of you tries to get clever, I'm a very good shot."

"Corporal Easton will never let you get us to the border," Kate said. "Bounty hunting is illegal here in Canada."

Crane snickered. "I'm willing to take my chances. The reward on the both of you is too much not to."

He released her and said, "Now, get that rope from my saddle."

She stepped away, and a man called from off to one side. "Crane! Drop that gun!"

Crane spun at the sound of the voice, ready to shoot, but a gun barked. The bullet caught Crane in the chest, and he was knocked backward to the ground.

Joe stepped forward and snatched the revolver from Crane's grip.

Crane was still breathing. Johnny walked in from the trees at the edge of the camp, and Crane's eyes were on him.

Johnny said to him, "I asked you once if you knew what kind of trouble you were bringing onto yourself.

Apparently you didn't."

"He does now," Joe said.

The front of Crane's shirt was torn where Johnny's bullet had cut into him, and the shirt was soaking with blood.

Crane opened his mouth to say something, but then he let out the air in his lungs, and he was gone.

Kate's hand was over her mouth. Joe went over to her and pulled her in for a hug.

He said, "Did he hurt you?"

Kate shook her head.

Joe looked over at Johnny. "I didn't know you were out there."

Johnny said, "Ain't a man alive can see me if I don't want to be seen."

Joe couldn't help but grin.

45

Easton was sitting in his office, with his left arm in a sling. Kate was in a chair across from his desk. Johnny stood by the stove, a cup of coffee in one hand, and Joe was beside him. Matt was perched on the edge of a second desk.

Easton said, "The doc says I should be fully back in action in a few weeks."

"I'm glad you weren't hurt worse than you were," Kate said, "and I feel bad that it happened because of Joe and me."

They had buried the body of Crane in the woods out behind the cabin. They had buried it deep, so no animals would dig it up.

"I feel a little odd about disposing of the body like we did," Kate said. "As strange as it might sound, considering I have been convicted of murder and sentenced to hang, I have never taken part in the actual killing of a person before."

"You didn't actually kill him," Joe said. "It was Johnny, making another one of them patented shots. The stuff dime novelists write about."

"Now, what'll happen to us? Where can we go?"

Easton said, "There's no reason why you can't stay right here."

"But you won't be assigned here forever."

He shrugged his good shoulder. "It won't make any

difference. You're Mister and Missus Joe O'Brien, right? No way to prove otherwise."

They heard a train whistle from outside. Easton glanced at a clock on one wall.

"That's the two-ten," he said, "looks like it's on time."

"That would be our train," Johnny said.

He and Matt had traveled light. Only what they could carry in two pair of saddlebags, and Johnny's rifle.

Joe and Kate walked with them to the train station.

Johnny stopped in front of the station and took a final look at the little town.

He said, "This place reminds me a little of McCabe Gap, back in the day. It's a nice little town. Except we had no train."

"It's a nice area. I like these mountains," Matt said, looking at Joe. "I think you've found the right place for you. And Easton is a good man. I think you can do well here."

Kate said, "But we're a long way from you and the family."

"Oh, it's not that far. We might see you from time to time."

Kate said to Johnny, "You saved my life years ago when that dreadful Indian kidnapped me. And now you did it again."

Matt was smiling. "One more thing to add to the legend."

Johnny gave him a look. "Don't you start."

Joe shook Johnny's hand, then pulled him in for a hug.

Joe said, "You take care of that family of yours."

"I will. And you take care of Kate."

Joe pulled Matt in for a hug and said, "Every time you use a ten-dollar word, you think of me."

Matt said, "I will. Every time."

Joe and Kate stood on the platform while Johnny and Matt climbed onto the train.

Joe said, "I rode across the country with them two, and now here they are. Watching my back. Just like old times."

Kate looked at him with a smile. "You're whole family is so special. You all are the stuff legends are made of."

"You're part of that family now. I hope you know that."

The train whistle sounded. The engine chugged. The conductor called out, "All aboard!"

Kate said, "I wonder if we'll ever find out who killed poor Eli. Or get our names cleared. It bothers me immensely that it's all hanging in front of us, unresolved."

Joe said, "Sometimes we can't always solve a problem, or right a wrong. Sometimes the best we can do is just move on from it."

The train began to move forward.

Kate took Joe's arm. She said, "So, where to now,

Mister O'Brien?"

Joe said, "Let's go home."

Made in the USA
San Bernardino, CA
11 January 2018